The Awari Paradox

The Awari Paradox

Don Dula

The Awari Paradox

For some, the idol was a symbol of hope.; for others, it was a device of destruction. It was physically small, but the pain it caused in many lives was large. On this fate-driven night, the idol was going to make its return. Nothing on earth would ever be the same again.

Sometimes things that are lost are not meant to be found.

Prologue

A storm was building as Marco looked over the bow of the ship. He worried the horrific storm was upon them.

"Marco! Marco!" Juan called out. Marco seemed to be in a trance. He had a look of deep worry on his face that Juan could not help but notice.

"Are you okay?" Juan moved closer to Marco as the boat swayed and bounced in response to the rough ocean.

"I'm worried about the approaching storm." Marco spoke while looking up at the night's sky. "Juan, we need to get the netting up and onto the boat before the worst of this storm hits us." Juan nodded in agreement. Both men ran to the stern of the ship. Marco turned to Juan and looked down, clenching his hands.

"Your sister. I want to make her proud. I used our life savings to buy this boat. I want to build a life for her and our kids. I love her so much." Juan put his hand on Marco's shoulder.

"You will. You're a good man. I will help you. Don't worry." Both men reached over the side of the boat trying to get a hold of the netting. The deck of the boat was getting slippery from the rain, it was coming down hard. The clouds passed over quickly, as the storm moved closer to the boat. It had started to rain even harder, the winds growing with intensity. The ocean swelled. The waves were now crashing over the boat with more and more force each minute.

"Juan, I can't get the net up! PULL HARDER!" Juan closed his eyes and pulled as hard as he could.

"We almost have it Juan…keep pulling!" A wave crashed into the boat causing both men to lose their footing, but they held the net, and slowly it moved.

"That's it, Marco. We almost have it!" Marco looked down into the net and for a split second thought he saw something. *What is that?* He saw a faint, light blue glow just under the water in the netting.

"Juan, pull as hard as you can, now." Marco could see in the distance a very large wave heading towards them. He thought to himself that, even in the dark, this wave looked massive. It instantly gave him cause to be worried, frightened. Juan backed up and pulled as hard as he could. Marco was now hanging partially over the boat. He pulled with all his might. The faint glow he saw earlier was now growing brighter in the dark ocean. Marco stood up and pulled the net while moving backwards. The wave was about a hundred yards out but rushing towards the boat.

"Now, Juan, pull!" They both pulled. The net made a strange sound as it flung up and onto the boat. Both men flew backwards, falling onto the deck. The glowing blue object landed and slid towards both men.

"What is that?" Juan whispered to Marco.

"I don't know. . .it looks like some kind of small statue. Like an idol." Both men eagerly reached for it. Just then, Marco looked at the bow of the ship to see the giant wave coming down on them. Marco grabbed the idol and stood up.

"Come on, Juan. We must get inside now." Juan jumped up, and both men ran. Marco could see the wave hit the bow just as he opened the door and pushed Juan inside the berthing. Marco ran in after Juan. He closed the door just as the water slammed against it. Both men fell into the near darkness. The only light was coming from the idol that was now in Marco's hand. The boat was now moving up and down with great force. Juan lost his balance and slammed his head on the counter, calling out to Marco for help. In the dark, Juan saw two small red dots. Lightning flashed outside.

"Marco, are you alright?" Juan called out. The red dots were moving towards him. He stood up, trying to make them out.

"Marco?" Juan yelled again. He heard a strange grumble and then, "Yes." The voice was deep, unrecognizable. It sounded almost as if two voices were speaking at once. He watched as the two red lights floated around the room. Lightning flashed again, and Juan saw Marco standing a few feet away from him. Marco's eyes were glowing blood red. He was grinning. Juan backed up in fear. Marco was holding the idol in one hand and a knife in the other.

"Oh, Juan, your fear is so invigorating!" Marco hissed, moving a few feet forward. Juan backed up into the corner and frantically searched the dark room for something to defend himself with, but there was no time. Marco rushed forward and stabbed him in the stomach. Juan cried out in agony as the thing that was once Marco

10

laughed. The ship rocked hard to the left. Juan struggled to pull a flare gun out of his belt.

"Please, forgive me!" he said as he shoved the gun into Marco's mouth and pulled the trigger. The thing's eyes shifted from red to Marco brown just before the blast. Both men fell over onto the floor from the force of the flare and the storm. The idol fell from Marco's hand and slid under a cabinet. The glow from the idol faded into the darkness. Blood from Juan's wound spread across the floor, pooling just short of the idol that no longer held its glow.

The following morning, helicopters from the Mexican navy located the boat now drifting off the coast of Mexico. The naval officers boarded and found Marco and Juan, lying on the floor in a pool of their shared blood. One of the officers radioed up to the helicopter.

"We located the men. I am sorry to have to inform Mrs. Alvarez that her husband and brother are both deceased." The officers looked down at the bodies.

"What do you think happened here?" the younger officer asked the older one.

"I don't know. The storm overcame them… But this boat should have made it through. The damage…it's, well, it is more than I would have thought possible. The officer stood in silent regret for such loss of young life. From what I understand, these two men were very close. This makes no sense to me." Hours later, the boat was brought into the harbor. Maria Alvarez and her young children were waiting. She stood at the dock, tears flowing down her face as her handkerchief hung limp in her hand. Her long, colorful dress fluttered as the wind whipped around her. She asked the children to return to their car. The older officer led her onto the ravaged boat, her long black hair shielding her face as cried. The bodies had been removed, but the blood

11

remained. She looked around the boat and asked the officer for a minute alone. Maria sat down and thought of her now dead husband and brother. She was now left with nothing but this wrecked boat to support her children. She had so many reasons to cry, but her gentle sobs were interrupted

"What is that?" she asked herself, as she knelt down. She reached under the cabinet and grasped a small statue. She shoved it in her pocket. It may be worth something. I'm going to need all the money I can get now, she thought to herself as she decided not to let the police know what she had found The officer returned and she quickly left the boat. Maria drove home in tears, her kids motionless and mute amid their loss. Once inside her tiny home, she lay down on her marriage bed and let the sobs overtake her. The idol glowed ever so slightly in her coat pocket.

Chapter 1

"Would you like peanuts or a snack pack?" Alex looked up at the smiling flight attendant.

"I think I will take the nuts. Oh, and a rum and coke please, Alex said, smiling back. Dark haired and seeming to be in his mid-20's, the attendant had winked and smiled at Alex so blatantly, Daniel couldn't help but notice. Alex was just about six feet tall, with dark hair and light green eyes that highlighted his Italian and Irish heritage. Daniel thought Alex was beautiful; unfortunately, so did other people. It didn't help that Alex was very outgoing and friendly. Up until the friendly attendant, Daniel had been looking out of the plane window thinking about Mexico. He now reached over Alex, signaling.

"Excuse me? He'll take the snack pack. The only nuts he will be getting on this trip are mines." The attendant looked a little miffed as he handed Daniel the snack pack. Alex laughed in surprise at Daniel's reaction. Daniel was usually soft spoken, quiet, and shy. "Honey, "Alex said, "You know I love you. I was just trying to get us the hook up on some goodies." Daniel laughed and rolled his eyes.

"I bet you were." Alex and Daniel held hands as the in-flight movie started. Alex leaned over and kissed Daniel on the cheek, then promptly fell asleep.

"Wake up Alex. We're about to land." Alex sat up and put his seat in the upright position. Daniel caressed the top of Alex's hand as they touched down on the runway, and Alex stood up to get his bags. The woman behind them had been watching their interaction.

"Oh, my lord! You two are sooo cute." She had a thick southern accent. "How long have you been together?" Alex smiled.

"Thank you. Going on five years." Daniel smiled at the woman as he moved closer to Alex.

Alex had met Daniel when he was a junior in high school. They had instantly hit it off and become quick best friends. It was during the course of their friendship that Alex realized just how much he loved Daniel. Loved him more deeply than just a platonic friend. It confused him at first. He'd never been attracted to another man before, but it felt right. Daniel had realized early on that he was gay, and his attraction to Alex had been instant. He liked how kind and non-judgmental Alex was. Daniel found that he could open up to Alex in ways he'd never done with anyone else in his life. Being with Alex brought him peace and helped him forget a troubled past.

Alex and Daniel walked out of the plane and into the airport.

"Wow! I can't believe we're here," Alex marveled. Daniel grabbed Alex's hand and started laughing.

"Honey, we need to get our bags."

"Oh, yeah," Alex said, laughing. He was awestruck at being in another country. They stood near the conveyer belt, waiting next to the other passengers surrounded by hustling and bustling. Daniel thought about all the great times he'd had with Alex over the years. His life had started with so much darkness, he couldn't have imagined he'd be at this point. Happy, in Mexico, with the man he loved. He looked over at Alex. *How did I get so lucky?* Daniel had asked himself that question a thousand times in the last five years. Alex spotted their bags and quickly ran to grabbed them.

"You thought my idea of getting a purple bag was crazy. Look how easy it was to spot." Daniel nodded in agreement as they walked outside to fetch a cab. They didn't have long to wait.

After giving the driver the address of the resort, they settled in for the short trip. A few minutes later, they gave the driver a generous tip and got their bags out of the trunk.

15

"Wow! Can you believe this place?" Alex spun in a circle while looking up at the ceiling of the resort. The lobby amazed him, all wood and very spacious. Colorful art was displayed on every wall. There was a large fountain in the middle of the lobby, giving the resort a tranquil feel. As they walked towards the concierge, a bellhop appeared. He handed them both a glass of champagne.

"Now this is living." Alex was impressed by the star treatment they were receiving. Daniel laughed as he sipped from his glass.

"Yeah, but we have to work the rest of our lives to pay for this trip." He was only half joking. Money issues had always worried him. Growing up, his dad had been a salesman. Not a very good one. He'd often lost jobs and moved Daniel from place to place without much notice. They had struggled. There were times when Daniel had gone days without eating solid food. He remembered the joy he felt when his dad finally landed a steady paying job at the local papermill. There was finally some stability in his life. He never wanted to be that vulnerable again. He tried not to let his past effect his relationship with Alex, but sometimes he couldn't stop his train of thought.

"Hey, you only live once." Alex's carefree voice brought Daniel back to the present. Their hotel room was all wood just like the lobby. The floors were marble and smooth. Alex touched the sheet on the bed and felt the high thread count. The room was decorated in a very modern way, neutral colors and simple furniture throughout the space making it seem bigger than it actually was. The air-conditioning cooled them as they walked around the room. Daniel put his bag down and went to shut the door. He turned around and hugged and kissed Alex.

"I'm so happy we're here."

"Me too," Alex smiled, holding Daniel's hand. A short while later, fatigue set in. They both put on more comfortable clothes and got into bed. They held each other tight as sleep overtook them.

Not far away, Maria Alvarez felt a tug at her shirt. She looked up to see her seven year old son trying to wake her.

"Mom, you told me to wake you up for work." She rubbed his head as she sluggishly sat up.

"Thank you, my boy."

"Mom? Why don't you stay home tonight?"

"We need to eat and more than ever I need to make us money." She said sadly, trying not to think of her late husband and brother.

"I know, Mom." Her son looked down in sadness.

"It's okay, baby. We'll be fine. I promise." He smiled and scampered out of the room. She gathered the beautiful garments she had spent the night before making. Her son ran back into her bedroom waving a piece of paper.

"Mom! You can sell my painting I just made!" he said excitedly.

"No, honey. You keep it. You worked so hard on it." She collected her creations and put them in the car. Her son laid the picture he made on top of them. She smiled at him and kissed him on his forehead.

"Almost forgot my coat. It's going to be chilly tonight." She grabbed it off the hook and jumped in the car. She waved goodbye to her children who were watching from the living room window. She cast her eyes downward, ashamed that she would soon be forced to sell some of her children's belongings. *I'm going to find a way to take care of them. I will not let my children starve*, she whispered to herself as she drove down the road.

"Alex! Get up. We have dinner reservations at eight." Daniel shook Alex lightly on the shoulder. It was a quarter past seven.

"Oh, shit!" Alex jumped up and ran to the shower. Daniel grabbed both of their shirts and started to iron them, remembering the times he'd had to iron his dad's clothes when he was too drunk to do so himself. A few minutes later, the phone on the dresser rang. Alex came dashing out of the bathroom in a towel and picked it up. He knew exactly who it was.

"Hi, Mom. We both made it fine. Yes, I will give Daniel your love. Yes, Mom, we're going to eat now." Alex smiled and rolled his eyes as Daniel continued ironing. Daniel waved to Alex.

"Daniel says hi, Mom." Alex took the phone away from his ear and put it out towards Daniel, who smiled and put the receiver to his ear.

"Hi, Mom. Yup, I'll take good care of Alex for you." Alex sat on the bed in his towel watching the exchange between Daniel and his mother. Daniel had lost his mom before they'd met. It warmed Alex's heart that Daniel had a connection to a mother figure again. Alex had grown up in the suburbs of Pennsylvania, his mother a teacher and his father a truck driver. He had a twin sister named Julie who he had been very close to until, in his first year of college, she had unexpectantly passed away from a rare cancer. The death of Julie had brought their family closer together in their grief, although his father had started working even more, keeping him away for longer periods of time and creating in Alex a responsibility to care for his mom in his father's absence. Daniel had become close to Alex's family quickly. He was around so much, Alex's mother started treating him like a second son. Daniel loved having a mother figure and a semblance of a normal family. It made him forget how dysfunctional his own family had been.

"I swear she likes you better than me." Alex commented as he started getting dressed. Daniel just smiled and handed Alex his pants.

They made their way out of the resort for dinner. The resort's Tiki torches were lit up, making the moonlight seem even brighter. They walked along the resort path towards the restaurant in silence, both contemplating their situations back at home.

"I'm so proud of you, Alex," Daniel said. "This promotion will mean more money, and you're finally getting the recognition you deserve for all your hard work."

"It will also mean longer hours and less time for us. That part I'm not happy about. But thank you." Alex kissed Daniels' hand.

"It's okay, Alex. I want you to be happy. You deserve this."

Alex stopped and looked at Daniel. Daniel was slightly shorter than him. His short, light brown hair was blowing softly in the wind. His eyes always seemed to be brooding, which was such a contrast from his docile personality. "I'm happy with you and the life we have. That means more to me than any promotion." Daniel blushed and clasped both of Alex's hands. They kissed as the moon glowed brightly behind them.

Maria Alvarez arrived at the resort and rushed into the employee entrance. Her manager walked up to her as she was taking off her coat.

"I am so sorry to hear about your husband and brother. You have my condolences." Her manager's sincerity almost made her break down. She held back the tears and thanked him.

"Do you need any help arranging your things?"

"I should be fine," she answered smiling.

"Okay. If you need anything, please, let me know." Her manager gave her shoulder a gentle squeeze then walked back to the lobby. Maria picked up her box of wares and took it to the display table reserved for her outside of the resort entrance. She had been selling her always popular unique and handmade items outside the resort for many years. Her table was one of the most successful in the resort town. Over the years, the money had helped her husband purchase his boat and add to their life savings, but during the past year her husband had drained those life savings on ever less profitable trips and ever more necessary boat repairs. She cried a little as she put her creations on the table. Her garments and jewelry were full of color and sparkled under the moon. She sat down and waited. She tried to steer her thoughts to her table. It was getting chilly. She put her on her coat and settled into her chair.

After their dinner, Daniel and Alex made their way back to the resort.

"I'm so full. I feel fat," Daniel groaned rubbing his protruding stomach.

"You do look a little fat," Alex laughed and rubbed Daniel's stomach. Daniel pushed Alex away playfully as they walked down the resort path to the surrounding courtyard.

"Cool! It's local vendors out tonight." Alex ran ahead of Daniel.

"Oh, man. Here goes all our money," Daniel groaned.

They saw all kinds of unique items and trinkets. Despite his earlier objection, Daniel found himself intrigued. He bought a lantern from one vendor and had started looking over items from the other vendors when he noticed a table full of beautiful jewelry. The woman selling the items looked up at him and smiled. Daniel approached the table.

"Hi! How are you tonight?" Daniel greeted her with enthusiasm. Maria responded with a smile but suddenly got misty eyed. The happiness of Daniel's

20

greeting had pierced her. Daniel, full of concern, went around the table and knelt in front of her.

"Are you alright?" He asked softly. He'd used this same tone many times while trying to wake his father after finding him passed out.

"My husband," was all she could get out before bursting into tears. Alex ran over after noticing Daniel kneeling in front of the woman.

"Is she okay?" Alex whispered to Daniel. Daniel stood up and looked at Alex with sadness.

"I think something happened to her husband."

"Do you want us to call someone for you?" Alex asked sympathetically. He thought she looked to be around the same age as his mom. She continued crying and shook her head no. Alex looked around trying to think of a way to help her.

"It's late, and it's getting cold. You shouldn't be out here alone, Miss." Alex hoped she would stop crying.

"This is how they make their money. I'm sure she would rather be with her family if she could." Daniel whispered to him. Maria wiped her eyes and looked up at them.

"You're right. I should be with my children right now. They lost someone, too," she reached for her jacket.

"What's your name, Miss? I can call you a cab," Daniel pulled his cell phone out.

"Maria Alvarez. And thank you, but I'll be okay. I have to pack my things up anyway before I can leave." Alex helped Mrs. Alvarez put on her coat.

"I'm so sorry for my outburst." She attempted to smooth her hair as she got her bearings.

21

"You have some really beautiful things, Mrs. Alvarez. I love these dresses."
Daniel was looking over her table. Alex moved to stand beside him. He felt so bad for
her. He knew how it felt to lose someone you loved. Painful emotions started to
resurface as he thought about his sister, Julie.

"We would like to buy two of these, if that's okay," Daniel pointed to a
cluster of ornate necklaces. Mrs. Alvarez smiled gratefully and started packaging the
items. After Daniel paid more than her asking price, Maria hugged him. He felt a
warm sensation as they embraced. As they released each other, he noticed a glowing
in her pocket. Maria followed his eyes to her pocket in shock. She reached in and
pulled out the little statue she had found on her husband's boat. It felt warm in her
hands.

It was getting warmer the longer she held it. A weird sensation came over
her, disorienting and unwelcome. She became nauseous.

"What is that? And how is it glowing?" Alex's eyes were wide with wonder.

Maria's hand was starting to burn. She thrust the idol towards Alex in a panic.

"Do you want to sell it?" Daniel was surprised at her reaction to the small
statue. She looked afraid. Maria shook her head no and started to pack up her things.
Alex took the statue from her and turned it over in his hand. It was warm and smooth
and did not burn him. It reminded him of something people from older civilizations
would worship. Like an idol. That's what it probably was. Some ancient idol. It had
intricate carvings on it and was light in his hands.

Daniel opened the bag of other items for Alex to place the idol in.

"I wonder how it glows in the dark," Alex asked, confused.

"I'm sure it's one of those glow-in-the-dark toys or something. I bet one of
her kids stuck it in her pocket." Daniel tried reassuring Alex as they made their way

22

back to their room. A sense of dread suddenly overcame Alex. He tried to shake it off as best as he could.

They arrived at their room and began to unwind. Daniel started to unpack the things they'd bought while Alex headed for the bathroom. He stood in the shower in quiet contemplation. He could not shake the worried feeling that was consuming him. He finished his shower and looked at his reflection in the mirror.

"What am I worried about?" Alex said to himself. "We are in a very safe resort. Nothing bad is going to happen." He didn't sound so sure of himself. He put a towel around his waist and left the bathroom. Daniel was already sleeping. Alex wrapped his arms around Daniel and pulled him close. He quickly drifted off to sleep.

Flashes of symbols danced in Alex's dream. People were screaming in the distance. Flames were moving down a stone hallway he couldn't recognize. In the center of the flames stood the idol, glowing blue with eyes a fiery red. Daniel appeared at the end of the burning hallway. Alex watched in horror as the flames reached Daniel, who began screaming in agony as the flames consumed him. Alex jolted awake, his body covered in sweat. Daniel remained asleep. Alex tried to get his breathing under control, but failed. He looked over at the bag of items they had bought and had a very uneasy feeling about the idol.

"Time to get up, Alex." Daniel said in a singsong voice. He was already up and dressed.

"You are too damn happy in the morning, Daniel." Alex grunted. Daniel laughed and pulled the bed covers off of him.

"We have a whole world to explore today, get up!" Alex sighed at Daniel but got dressed. They had activities planned for that whole day.

First was a trip to a private island. Then they zip-lined and drank exotic mixed cocktails. They enjoyed the sights and each other's company until the sun went down, but Alex could not shake the feeling that there was something wrong with the little statue, the idol, in the bag in their room.

"Hey, babe, would you mind if I mailed that statue back home?"

"No, but why can't you just take it home when we leave?" Daniel asked, confused as he undressed for a shower.

"I want Ron to look at it." Ron was Alex's close friend from college. Ron had transferred from NYU to the small college in Pennsylvania Alex attended. They were both what you would call nerds, so they became fast friends. Ron was like a brother to him, even though they couldn't have looked more different from each other. Ron was taller than Alex, black, wore wire rimmed glasses, and had mid-back-length dreadlocks. But Ron was the most intelligent person he'd ever met. He had moved back to New York, and was now an expert in ancient history and civilizations. He loved artifacts and knew more about ancient cultures than anyone Alex could think of. If anyone could identify the idol, it would be Ron. Alex was sure he wouldn't mind. He visited so often, Alex and Daniel had given him a spare key to their place.

"Hun, it's just a toy. I'm sure it's not real." Daniel was always the voice of reason, but this time Alex could not agree. There was something strange, even wrong, about that idol. He was intent on finding out what it was. He didn't want it in the room with them any longer.

"Maybe so, but I still want to ship it home. Ron can pick it up, take a look at it." "

"Okay… yeah, I think you are thinking too deep about this, though." Daniel said as he walked towards the bathroom. Alex couldn't explain to Daniel the sense of foreboding that overcame him whenever he was near the idol. He couldn't even tell him about the nightmare he'd had last night. There were no words to describe it without having him sound like a madman. Daniel emerged from the shower a few minutes later and started getting ready for dinner.

"I'm going to pack up the idol and take it to the lobby, mail it back home now. I'll be right back." Daniel walked up to Alex and pulled him close.

"Hun, Try to relax, okay? I love you, so much." Alex hugged Daniel tight and took in his scent. It was just the comfort he needed to calm his nerves, even if just a little.

"I love you, too. I will relax, I promise. See you in a bit."

Alex walked downstairs to a gift shop in the lobby that had mail services. A feeling that something was crawling on him made him stop and look around. He felt like he was being watched, out of the corner of his eye, he thought he saw something red and glowing. He ignored it, walked into the shop and bought a box, postage, and some wrapping paper and prepared the idol for shipping. A young Mexican woman waited behind the counter. Alex opened his wallet.

"Would you mind mailing this for me?"

"Not at all," she said pleasantly. He watched her put the box into the mail bin.

"Thank you," Alex said, walking away from the desk. Alex noticed that people in the lobby were staring at him as he walked towards the elevators.

Why are people looking at me? He thought to himself as a couple in their early twenties walked over to him.

"Where did you get your contacts? Those are so cool, man!"

"Contacts?" Alex self-consciously touched his eyes.

"How did you get them to glow like that? It looks painful." The couple walked away shaking their heads in wonder. Alex searched the lobby frantically for a bathroom. Panic started to rise inside him. Something was terribly wrong. He spotted a bathroom sign further down the lobby. He nearly ran to it.

"WHAT THE HELL?" he screamed into the bathroom mirror. His eyes were ice blue and glowing.

"Oh my god," he whimpered in fear staring into his reflection in disbelief. He could hear his heart in his ears thundering like African drums. *What's happening to me?* He pushed himself away from the mirror and ran back to the elevator bank. He ran so fast that he knocked someone over as he hit the elevator button.

"Sorry!" His body was shaking as the elevator rose. He yanked his room door open. Part of him thought it was all a dream. He needed to talk to Daniel. Level-headed Daniel would be able to make sense of all of this.

He walked into the room and chaos greeted him. It looked like it had been ransacked. Their clothes were strewn on the floor and shredded. The TV was knocked over and there were scratch marks across the dresser. The bed had been ripped apart.

"DANIEL!" Alex yelled out for his love, who was nowhere to be seen. He ran through their room looking for him, all the while yelling out his name. In in the bathroom were all of Daniels things on the floor, but no Daniel.

"Oh, no!" Alex's mounting panic ripped through him. Suddenly the lights went out. His head jerked to the side when he heard a voice in the dark.

"Where is it? We can't sense it anymore." The voice didn't belong to Daniel. A cold fear shot through Alex's heart. Whoever the voice belonged to was looking for something. Alex knew immediately it had something to do with the idol. Alex slowly stepped out of the bathroom to feel his way back towards the main room. His eyes hadn't adjusted to the darkness yet.

"Where is Daniel?" In the dark, Alex could see two red dots glowing. They were eye level with him. Before he could try to decipher what was happening, hands were around his neck.

"Where is Daniel?" Alex choked out as the hands tightened around his throat. He still could not see who or what was choking him. A sliver of light came through the window, shining on the person choking him, although "person" was the wrong word to describe what he saw. Alex's eyes bulged out of his head at the sight of Mrs. Alvarez. Her face was contorted in a grotesque, unnatural way. Her mouth was twisted to one side and her eyes glowed red. Spit was running out of her mouth, her teeth seemingly sharpened. Mrs. Alvarez was no longer human, but a creature of some kind. Alex was losing consciousness from the strength of her grip on his neck. His eyes caught movement behind the creature in the light.

Alex watched as a knife came through the creature's chest.

"RRRRRAAAAAAAAA!" It screamed out in rage, throwing Alex to the floor. From this position, Alex watched Daniel push the creature up against the wall. A rush of relief passed through him. Daniel was alive.. Banging erupted on the hotel room door.

"What is going on in there?" A male voice yelled. Alex's throat was raw, he couldn't answer. He turned his attention back to Daniel, still struggling with the creature. Daniel was on the thinner side and even if Mrs. Alvarez had not been some possessed thing, she was probably stronger than Daniel. She weighed at least fifty more pounds than him. Daniel dodged a punch from the creature, only to fall right into the creature's grasp. Alex watched in terror as the creature lifted Daniel up in the air. Alex tried to stand. Up in the air, Daniel caught his gaze.

"I love you, Alex," he said softly and then plunged his hand into the knife wound in the creature's chest. The creature screeched in pain, and its blood flowed a glowing blue, spreading up Daniel's hand and throughout the creature's body. The blood was an energy encompassing Daniel's whole body.

"NOOOOO!" Alex's throat was on fire. Tears streamed down his eyes as he pulled himself to his feet to get to Daniel. The creature started to yell out in agony. Alex ran towards it, reaching out for Daniel. Just as his hand was upon Daniel, a flash of bright light blinded him.

"ALEX!" Daniel screamed before another flash of light assaulted Alex's eyes. By the time the light died out, both the creature and Daniel were gone.

"Daniel?" Alex was traumatized. His mind could not wrap itself around what had just happened. The hotel room lights had come back on. He heard the room door open but he couldn't move. He couldn't concentrate on anything but the last image of Daniel glowing blue. The resort manager found him curled up on the floor crying.

Chapter 2

The next few days were a blur for Alex. The morning following Daniel's death, Alex was taken to the police station to make a statement. There was no evidence of a murder. The local police concluded that Daniel had walked out on Alex after a fight. A lover's quarrel. The hotel guests told the police they heard Alex and Daniel screaming each other's names and throwing things around. The evidence suggested they'd had a major fight and nothing else. Alex was a zombie. He could not believe or make sense of what had happened. Was it real? Was he going crazy? Did all of this have to do with the idol? Questions flew around his head constantly.

Alex boarded the plane back to the states a few days later. He dreaded telling Daniel's family and his own about what happened. He didn't even know what he was going to say. Daniel disappeared into a glowing white light? A woman-creature hybrid had killed him? He sounded crazy even to himself. He looked out of the window of the plane, his vision blurry as tears flowed down his face.

"I miss you, Daniel." The plane flew through the clouds on its way back to New York. Without Daniel.

It had been a long day at the office. Alex tried to reintegrate to his normal routine. He'd gotten a promotion before he and Daniel had gone on vacation. His boss had been very understanding of Daniel's death and had given Alex a week off for bereavement. It had been six weeks since then and Alex was going over everything that had happened all over again. He missed Daniel every minute of every day. He needed to understand. It was driving him crazy. Work was a small distraction, but his mind could not rest with so many unanswered questions. One day as he was doing laundry, he pulled out a card from his pants pocket. It was the card from the detective who'd closed Daniel's case. He called and got the detective's receptionist. After asking for any updates, she informed him that Daniel's case file had been sent to the states shortly after his disappearance. She couldn't give him any more details than that. Alex called every police district in New York, until he reached the one that received Daniel's file. After trying for a week straight to get some answers, he kept getting the run around. Alex was exhausted. Physically, mentally, and emotionally.

It had now been two months since Daniel's disappearance. Alex was in a daze. He no longer cared about figuring out the connection between Daniel's disappearance and the idol. It had sat in the box he'd mailed it in for weeks. He had never gotten the chance to call Ron about it. It had never glowed again once he got home, and he never touched it again. He figured whatever secrets it held had disappeared with Daniel. Time continued to pass. He gathered Daniel's things to sell after months of crying into his shirts. It was too painful to see them every day. He held the idol in his hand one more time before putting a one dollar sticker on it, and sold it at a yard sale. He vaguely remembered who bought it. Daniel's father never returned his calls after he told him what happened. He gave the money from the yard sale to a favorite charity of Daniel's.

Alex was finally able to sleep a full night after almost three months. He thought maybe he was starting to pull himself out of his grief when he received a phone call from a Detective Granger about Daniel's case. He wanted to meet Alex in person and discuss something he'd found. A newfound sense of hope flowed through Alex.

Granger opted to meet Alex at his house rather than have Alex come down to the station. Alex didn't question this and waited impatiently for the detective to arrive. He had worried that the growing thunderstorm would stop Granger from coming over, but Granger had called to confirm that morning. He seemed even more eager to meet than when they'd first spoke. His voice was deep and rough. Like he smoked and drank regularly. Alex hoped Granger would help more than the investigators in Mexico had.

Alex leaned against the sliding glass door of his patio. The rain was steady and growing with intensity. The lightning flashed and seemed to shroud his house in light. He unbuttoned his dress shirt down to his belt. His nerves were on edge. He had poured himself a glass of wine as soon as he'd walked into the door. The wine spilled down his chin as he sloppily drank from the glass. He didn't even care. Alex was getting tipsy. He shook his head, feeling dizzy. The storm was beautiful as it moved across the darkened field behind the house. He slid the patio door open and took in the storm's full effects. The wind was strong. A wild gust of wind blew his shirt back as the rain fell onto his exposed chest. His fingers fumbled as he tried to take his tie completely off. His fingers weren't cooperating, so his tie hung around his neck, feeling like a leash.

Alex wanted to have a clear head when Granger came, so he made his way towards the bathroom. A sense of apprehension overcame him as he thought about meeting the detective. Alex thought he may have made a mistake by agreeing to let him come there.

Alex had figured out the cop was gay from their initial conversation. Granger hadn't blatantly flirted with Alex, but he was a little more friendly than the conversation warranted. To Alex's disgust, he didn't stop him. He figured a little flirting with Granger would help him prioritize Daniel's case. He had no doubt the police were working on hundreds of unsolved cases, and didn't want Daniel's to be one of the ones that ended up like that.

In the shower, the soapy water cascaded down Alex's body as he washed his hair. He couldn't help but think of how Daniel loved to mold his hair into a Mohawk while they showered together. They would laugh and hug each other close as the warm water rushed down their backs.

Alex picked up a picture of Daniel off their dresser as he toweled himself dry. There was so much he missed about Daniel. So much more they had yet had to explore in life together. Now Daniel was gone, leaving Alex with questions and regrets. He refocused himself and got dressed, determined to find out what happened to the love of his life. He hoped this meeting tonight would shed more light on everything.

Alex purposely wore a form-fitting flannel shirt, tight black jeans, and black hiking boots. He walked down the steps from the bedroom when the doorbell rang. *It's for Daniel*, he told himself as he answered the door. With wine in hand, and shirt partially open, he pasted on a fake sultry smile. He knew this was a desperate attempt at getting answers, but he didn't care.

Granger stood in the doorway for a moment appraising Alex. After a few seconds, he walked into the house. Although Alex had zero interest in anyone besides Daniel, he could not help but find the detective incredibly sexy, taller than he had expected. He had a tan complexion and was a bit stocky. His eyes were dark brown and intense. Granger walked in like he had been there before. Light reflected off his badge as he walked in with a pad in one hand. He smelled strange to Alex, but he ignored that and tried to calm down. Granger threw his small notepad on the floor as soon as Alex started to close the door. Before he could get the door closed all the way, Granger rushed towards Alex, pinning him against the wall. Alex felt a small trickle of fear run through him. Flirting was one thing, but there was no way he was doing anything physical with Granger. Granger obviously did not come over to talk about Daniel's case. Alex felt stupid as he put his hands against Granger's chest, putting some space between their bodies.

"Wait! We should talk about the case first. I, I have some questions." Alex stuttered trying to fight Granger off him. He felt Granger's hand go around his waist. Granger then grabbed Alex by the arms and pushed them up above his head. *Damn! This guy is getting out of hand*, Alex thought in irritation. He grabbed Alex's thick jet black hair, and looked deep into his eyes. Not only was he not getting any answers about Daniel's case, now he was being aggressively groped.

Alex felt frozen in place. Panic crept its way up his spine as he realized he was getting aroused. His body was betraying him. The last thing he wanted was for any man besides Daniel to touch him. Alex couldn't fathom what was happening to his body. There was a sound at his door, forcing his gaze that way. He looked over his shoulder and for a split second thought he saw a shadow standing in the door frame. Inside the shadow a grin appeared with jagged teeth. Voices trailed into his ear. Suddenly, Alex heard what sounded like hundreds of people screaming in agony. He flinched as pain shot through his ear from the screaming. The jagged teeth started to fall to the ground in front of him, one by one. The lightning flashed, and the shadow and sound of people screaming were gone.

His mind was reeling. He was terrified and in pleasure at the same time. Words were being whispered directly into his mind. Words he'd never heard before, words he couldn't understand. Alex could feel Granger's excitement through his jeans. He could not move or speak. His breath caught as he felt anticipation building inside him. It wasn't a real emotion. Now Alex was getting terrified. Something was controlling him from the inside out. His eyes danced around the room as he tried to think of a way to escape whatever hold or trance he was in. Granger let Alex's arms go and walked over to pick up the glass of wine he had knocked out of Alex's hand when he'd jumped him. There was still some left in the glass. He took a gulp of the wine and held it in his mouth. He stood in front of Alex's body, which was frozen in place against the wall, and brought his lips towards him. He leaned in to kiss Alex. Alex felt his mouth opening involuntarily as Granger spit the wine from his mouth into Alex's. He could feel it rush down his throat. Some of the wine escaped Alex's mouth and fell down his lips and chest. Granger licked the wine off him. Alex felt his eyes close in ecstasy. He tried to fight it, but he couldn't.

Granger spread Alex's legs farther apart and inserted his body in between them. He grabbed Alex's hair and moved his head slightly to the left. Alex felt warm lips start to suck and bite gently around his neck. Alex moaned and squirmed. Granger started sucking Alex's bottom lip. Alex opened his eyes and looked at Granger's lips. They were smeared in blood. The whole bottom of his face was completely dripping in blood.

I'm hallucinating. This can't be real, Alex thought to himself. He hadn't been sleeping well since Daniel's death, maybe his mind was playing tricks on him. Alex tried to rationalize everything that was happening, but couldn't.

Again, Alex tried to force Granger off him but to no avail. Granger's eyes suddenly turned a solid black. He gazed at Alex and he could have sworn his soul was being pulled into those eyes. Alex struggled to move, fear compelling him to keep trying to break free. Granger bit Alex's lip hard enough to warn him that he was in control.

Granger rubbed his face against Alex's. Alex could feel and hear the blood from both of their bodies pumping between them as if they were one. Granger plunged his tongue deep into Alex's mouth. The sensation of levitation came over Alex as he sucked on Granger's hot tongue. Inside he felt nauseous. He hated having Granger touch him, and was disgusted at his own response to Granger. Alex tried to concentrate his thoughts to regain control of his body and his mind, but he couldn't think straight. Granger's tongue was flicking in and out of Alex's mouth, suffocating him. Suddenly, Granger stopped and stared directly into Alex's eyes.

The front door was still open and the storm outside was raging on. The lightning flashed and the roar of the thunder echoed throughout the hallway. Granger slammed the front door, shaking the walls. Alex took a breath as his heartbeat pounded in his chest. Granger put his hand on Alex's shoulder and pushed him down to his knees.

Anxiety was coursing through Alex's body. He did not want to take contact any further with Granger, but he still had no control over his movements. Alex closed his eyes in defeat as Granger shoved his thumb into his mouth. Alex heard the sound of a zipper being unzipped. Alex looked up into Granger's black eyes, pleading for him to stop. Granger smiled and looked down at Alex with a mischievous smile.

"You're going to be my little lamb tonight," Granger growled and pushed his thumb deeper down Alex's throat. That jolted Alex into action. He somehow found enough strength to grab at Granger's leg. It took almost everything in him to get a good grip. Granger's eyes went wide. His thick hand cocked back and came down, smacking Alex in the face, hard. Alex couldn't scream. He took the pain and watched in horror as Granger's eyes went from black to blood red.

He tried again to get his hands to move, but it was like Granger was holding his wrists tight without even touching him. Granger's fingernails started to grow in front of Alex's surprised eyes. *What am I seeing?* Alex's thoughts were dispersed. Nothing was making sense. So much was happening so fast, his mind couldn't keep up. Long, black nails pushed through Grangers fingertips.

Alex looked up into Granger's red eyes in fear. He didn't know what was going to happen next. Granger's deranged eyes grew redder, and his mouth morphed into a sinister grin. Granger's eyes were burning into Alex's soul.

"I'm going to be ready soon, then it will be over," Granger's voice taunted. *What the fuck does that mean?* Alex's fear level was at an all-time high. He was helpless, at the mercy of a monster. He struggled to move so hard, his veins were bulging out his neck. Alex was tired from the exertion of trying to move. Granger bent down towards him, looking at his mouth. Feeling was returning to Alex's limbs. Just as Granger got within an inch of Alex's face, Alex slammed his forehead into Granger's chin. He instantly got dizzy, but adrenaline rushed through him. Granger grunted in pain and stumbled a few steps back. Alex jumped up and attempted to run. He didn't make it far before hands grabbed him and threw him across the floor. Granger was on top of him before he could react.

"SHIT!" Alex screamed in shock as Granger jumped on top of him. *How the hell did he move so fast? What the hell is he?* As if he heard Alex's thoughts, Granger looked him directly in the eyes.

"You're a feisty one. I like that." Granger's eyes kept shifting from completely black to searing red. He was so heavy. Alex struggled to move, but Granger held him pinned to the floor. Granger used one of his long nailed hands to rip his shirt completely off his body. His large chest was tattooed everywhere. There was no skin that hadn't been touched by ink. Alex noticed spikes pierced through Granger's nipples. He cringed. Something about the tattoos caught Alex's attention. Intricate and complex symbols were drawn all over Granger. Alex realized he'd seen those markings before, but he couldn't remember where he'd seen them.

With his free hand, Granger started rubbing his chest and licking his lips seductively. His right eye shifted and moved to the right side of his head. Alex was frozen in shock. He couldn't believe what he was seeing was true. Granger looked up at the ceiling.

"Enough foreplay. You're going to get what you deserve tonight!" His voice was so deep that it rumbled. Alex tried to come out of the shock he was in and get Granger off of him. He was still pinned to the floor. Alex fought hard to loosen himself from Granger's grip. He thought he felt Granger start to move off, but he was dead wrong. Watching in terror, Alex saw something trying to push through Granger's skin.

Something was trying to get out of him. Granger's body started contorting. Alex used that small bit of movement to free one of his legs from underneath Granger.

The thing trying to get out of him was getting stronger. Alex saw the outline of a hand pushing against Granger's stomach.

"AAAAAAHHHHHH!" Granger screamed in agony at the hand trying to push through him. Alex scrambled to his feet just as the lights went out. The only light in the room was from the lightning outside. Granger screamed again as spit flew out his mouth. He slammed his fists on the living room floor. His long, black nails scratched across the wood. Alex hurriedly crawled back towards the staircase. He was almost there when he heard a voice. A voice he hadn't heard in months. It stopped him dead in his tracks. Alex was on all fours crawling towards the steps. He turned to face Granger, only to see the outline of a face inside of Granger's stomach.

"Run, Alex! Run now!"

Alex screamed in horror and pushed himself backwards up the steps. He'd recognized that voice immediately. It was Daniel's.

Chapter 3

Still in shock, Alex ran up the stairs, tripping the whole way up to the second floor. The hallway was completely dark. He ran into the small table in the hallway, knocking everything off of it. The thunder was so loud. The rain was hitting the windows full force. Alex knew he needed to find a weapon. *Daniel was inside of that thing*, Alex thought, getting sick to his stomach. Alex thought of Daniel's funeral and visiting Daniel's grave. This whole time Daniel had not been at rest. He was in that thing. Alex found his way into his bedroom and took a breath. He needed to figure this out. He heard movement downstairs from Granger, but so far no noise from the staircase being mounted. His house was surrounded by trees. He had thought it was serene when he'd bought it, now he regretted it. No one would be able to hear him scream.

"Shit! This is so fucked up!" Alex silently fumed rummaging through his drawers. Alex stopped suddenly. He could now hear Granger coming up the stairs, banging on the staircase walls and yelling.

"You can't get away. Give in and I'll make this a nice experience for you. You may even like it!" Granger's rumbling voice said temptingly.

Alex ignored him and kept looking around his room for something to defend himself with. He couldn't concentrate enough to figure out where he recognized those symbols from. His mind was in a state of chaos.

"Found you!"

"FUCK!" Alex screamed and ran towards the other side of the bedroom. The only thing between him and Granger was the bed. In the darkness, all Alex could see were Granger's glowing red eyes. He knew that fucker was smiling without even seeing it.

"Ready to get your soul taken tonight?" Granger asked nicely. It was as if he'd asked whether Alex wanted a glass of lemonade. Alex's breath caught in his throat as Granger pushed the bed slowly toward him. *He's trying to pin me against the wall!*

"I guess I should thank you for bringing us here. We have grown so strong from all of the souls we captured." Granger was talking as he moved the bed closer and closer to Alex. "What are you talking about?" Now Alex was even more confused. "Who is 'us'?" Granger smiled devilishly as he pushed the bed up to Alex's hips.

"Us. The souls inside. You brought the Awari to such a sinful city. We added so many souls to the collective. I truly love New York." Alex stopped thinking about the bed pressing against him and focused. His mind was reeling.

"What the hell is an Awari?" He tried to think about what he'd brought home with him. He'd only brought home his and Daniel's belongings. He remembered buying some stuff from the vendors outside the resort. Alex wracked his brain trying to remember. They had purchased jewelry and. . .the idol! Alex knew immediately that that was what Granger was referring to. Ever since he'd come into contact with it, he felt a dark presence. It was called an Awari. But that didn't explain what exactly an Awari was.

"I can see from your face, you do know. What you thought was a little trinket was actually our way here. It was the key to revive our master. Anyone who touches it calls us into their path. The longer you touch it, the better chance we have of sucking in your soul." Alex thought about Mrs. Alvarez and how she'd completely changed that day in Mexico. She'd had the Awari for who knows how long before they'd bought it from her. Her soul had been taken and replaced with something evil and menacing. Alex had a thought and panicked. *I touched the Awari!* He had held it in his hands for at least a minute and then touched it again when he wrapped it to ship it home. But why hadn't he changed? What made him different from Mrs. Alvarez? Why hadn't it affected him like it had affected Granger? Alex didn't have time to think about the answers to those questions. The bed scratched against the wood floor. Granger looked directly at Alex and spoke in a low tone. His voice sounded like many voices speaking at once.

"We are in many people already. The Awari awakens us in certain people. We are everywhere. You only need to touch the Awari once and it changes your aura. Makes us able to see you. It pulls us to you like a beacon. I can see it even in the dark. Your aura is that of the Awari." Granger started to climb onto the bed.

"You will never be able to hide. You know how we capture innocent souls? We kill you during your most frightened state." He licked his lips in ecstasy.

"It is so delicious. I can taste your fear. So much raw energy." If Alex was understanding everything right, the Awari had awakened something dark. And those dark things have the ability to take souls and turn those people into whatever the hell Granger was. If all of that was true, the only way to stop this from happening was to destroy the Awari. That was going to be damn near impossible since he'd sold the Awari at a yard sale. There was no time to think of that now, Alex had to act, quick. Granger was on the bed looking down on him. He'd said he needed to wait until Alex was full of fear to steal his soul. Alex had to somehow convince himself not to be afraid. That was like counting sand. Alex took a breath and closed his eyes. The only way to ease his fear was to think of him and Daniel together. They'd shared so many beautiful, blissful times together. He felt his fear slipping away and being replaced by warmth. Daniel. The love of his life. He was somehow trapped inside of Granger. Alex knew that he had to free Daniel before he destroyed the Awari, or he'd be lost forever.

His only chance of finding a weapon, was to make it to the bathroom. There was no way he could take on Granger in a fight. Alex was no fighter, but even if he was, Granger seemed to have superhuman strength. He didn't stand a chance against

44

him. The only thought in Alex's mind was Daniel. He could help him, even being trapped inside Granger.

"DANIEL! CAN YOU HEAR ME? HELP ME PLEASE!" Alex screamed for Daniel in a panic. He could see Granger stall and start to struggle to get control of his body. Daniel was fighting against him. Alex worried for Daniel's safety inside that beast. His fear came back immediately.

"Oh yeah! You will be fully absorbed soon," Granger moaned and closed his eyes. Alex knew this was his only shot at escape. As soon as Granger's eyes closed, he dashed into the bathroom and quickly closed and locked the door. He could hear his own breathing. It was erratic and coming out in short bursts. The bathroom had no windows, but it did have something Alex could use. Granger was at the door now.

"Come on out and play," Granger's voice had changed. It seemed almost soothing. It was like a lullaby. Alex felt himself reaching to unlock the bathroom door. He shook his head fast and hard to snap out of it. He had to get back in control. It was clear that whatever Granger was, he had the ability to influence and control someone's mind. Alex searched through the bathroom cabinets, trying to block out Granger's singsong voice. He came up with an idea. It was flimsy at best, but should still work. He put the spray bathtub cleanser, the hairdryer, and the nail clippers on the toilet. He grabbed a bucket and filled it with water.

"What are you doing little lamb?" Granger's voice rumbled through the door. Alex ignored him as best as he could and used the nail clippers to strip the rubber off the hair dryer cord. With the wires exposed, he plugged in the hair dryer. Granger was pounding on the door at this point.

Alex kept ignoring him. He pounded harder and harder on the door, making it shake from the force. Alex knew he only had one shot at this, so he needed to time it perfectly. He stood up on the toilet just as Granger pushed the door off its hinges.

Alex quickly sprayed the cleanser in its eyes. It screamed unnaturally and fumbled backwards a few steps. Alex reached down and picked up the plunger. He rammed the handle of the plunger into its left eye. More screams. He emptied the bucket of water on the floor and threw the hair dryer on the floor. There was a loud pop and then sparks crackled. Granger started shaking and grabbing his face. His painful moans were louder than the thunder outside. Granger growled and fell onto the bathroom sink. Alex watched for a second before jumping as hard as he could from the toilet to the hallway. He prayed he would clear the bathroom floor in his leap or he too would be electrocuted. He barely made the jump to the hallway. He could see Granger starting to get up.

"Shit!" Alex said under his breath as he ran down the dark hallway and down the stairs. He ran through the house to the garage. He had to get to his car. He quickly swiped his keys that were on the key ring in the garage.

Alex could hear Granger coming down the hallway. He quickly ran to the car. He was so nervous. His hands were shaking as he tried to hit the unlock button on his key fob. He heard Granger yelling out for him, his voice getting closer. The garage door was down. Alex kept pushing the garage door button over and over.

"COME ON GODDAMN IT!" Alex practically beat the remote to death.

"Thank god!" The garage door started to lift up slowly. He turned the front lights on, and the creature was standing in front of the car.

"AHHHH!" Alex almost jumped out of his skin. Granger's eyes were blood red. His nails had grown even longer.

"Enough games!" he yelled as he started to climb on the hood of the car. The garage door was halfway up.

"FUCK IT!" Alex yelled as he slammed on the accelerator. The car crashed into the garage door and quickly flew back.

The impact shattered the back windows. The garage door was badly dented and stuck in mid-air. The creature had been jolted but he was still climbing on the hood of the car. He reached out towards the driver's side window. Alex pressed down hard on the gas pedal. He could hear the wheels of the car grinding in the garage floor. The tires were screeching so loud that he could barely hear the thunder outside. The garage door creaked then gave way. Alex floored it. The head of the creature hit the dented garage door as the car accelerated. Alex could see the creature land on the ground as he drove faster and faster away from his house. The rain was coming down hard and he could barely see anything. But the only thing on Alex's mind was finding that Awari. He had to free Daniel first. He didn't even know where to start, he just knew he had to do it now. He thought long and hard about who he'd sold it to. That day had been such a blur. Adrenaline, fear, and anger were coursing through him. He was more focused now than he'd been since Daniel's death. He suddenly remembered who he'd sold the Awari to. He prayed that the person still had the artifact. More importantly, he prayed he was still alive.

Chapter 4

He drove aimlessly for about an hour, not knowing exactly where he was going. He just didn't want to stop in one spot for too long. He pulled over on the highway and turned the lights off. The words of that thing repeated over and over in his head. *You only need to touch the Awari once and it changes your aura.* His aura had changed. Alex remembered seeing a special on the Discovery Channel about the aura. The scientist said that the aura is the electrical field generated by the body. None of this seemed real to Alex. He didn't even know if that Granger creature was actually real. But if it was, Alex suspected it wouldn't be long before it found him again.

He searched for his phone and called his friend Chris. The phone rang for what seemed like forever before he picked up. The lightning was getting worse. Rain was coming down so hard that he couldn't see anything. The windshield wipers were useless in this storm.

"Hello?" Chris's sleepy voice answered the phone. Chris was a friend of his from college. He knew almost everyone and was always the life of the party. Alex knew he could get the information he needed from him.

"Hey Chris! It's Alex. Sorry, I know it's late. I have a question. Do you remember when I had that yard sale?"

"Yes, why, what's up?" he yawned loudly into the phone. Alex wanted to tell him what had just happened to him, but he knew Chris would think he was crazy. Alex casually mentioned the artifact, trying to sound as nonchalant as he could.

"I sold you a little statue. It was an artifact that I brought back with me from Mexico. I thought it was a little gimmicky at the time, but I would love to get it back for sentimental reasons. Daniel bought it for me." Alex added the last bit on for sympathy. His voice had cracked saying Daniel's name. He couldn't think about Daniel being inside of the that creature.

"I would love to give it back to you, but I don't have it. Jared's the one that actually bought it. It gave me the creeps so I never touched it." Chris grunted and Alex heard movement in his background. It was like he was shifting around or sitting up. Alex had only met Jared a few times before. He hadn't seen him in years, though. He and Daniel had met Jared at an art show. Alex was immediately taken by Jared's knowledge of the art on display. He'd pegged him as a bored rich kid who was just floating through life. Even his appearance gave the impression he lived a posh life. His stark white hair had been perfectly coifed. His attire had probably cost more than Alex and Daniel's rent. His dark brown eyes seemed like they hid a lot of secrets, but Alex and Daniel had taken to him quickly as they discussed art. He seemed very down to earth and was actually pretty funny. Hopefully Jared still remembered him.

"Damn. You think he would mind giving it back to me? Could you ask him?"

"I can't," Chris's voice was clearer now.

"Why not?" Alex asked feeling frustrated.

"We went to the club last week. After about twenty minutes, he ran out of the club screaming. I don't know what drug he took, but I have not seen or heard from him since." Alex closed his eyes and tried to calm down. The Awari had gotten to him. He just knew it. Chris started talking again.

"All he kept saying is that 'they're' after him. The last I heard was he locked himself in his condo and refused to come out." A horn blew and a truck pulled up to Alex's bumper. He did a quick glance behind him but kept his attention on his phone call.

"Thanks, Chris. Where does Jared live? Maybe I can get him to talk to me." Alex was grasping at straws.

"Hold on," Chris rattled off an address. Alex didn't have a pen, so he repeated the address a few times to memorize it. Just as he was about to tell Chris thank you, the truck behind him slammed into the back of his car.

"WHAT THE FUCK!" The car catapulted forward. The horn on the truck blew loud as it pushed the car into the guard rail. The car suddenly shut off. Everything was happening so fast. Alex turned the key over and over and could not get the car started again. He tried to open the driver's side door as the truck reversed. It inched backwards then started coming towards the driver's side door. Alex panicked and jumped into the passenger seat. To his shock, the passenger side door was blocked by the guardrail. He couldn't get out that way. He could hear the metal of the car starting to crunch and bend. The truck was trying to kill him by slowly crushing the car. His heart was beating faster than he could imagine. He tried to calm down to figure out how to get out of his car. An idea popped into his head as the truck reversed again. He quickly lay down in the passenger side seat on his back. He put his boots up to the passenger side window and started kicking. He kept kicking over and over as the car smashed further and further into the guardrail. For a split second, he thought about trying to roll the window down. He needed the car to start for that to happen.

The horn on the truck wailed as it smashed into Alex's car again. He got whiplash from the truck continuously ramming into his car. Fear was taking over him again. He remembered the creature saying that fear was how they killed their victims. Alex tried to control his fear, but it was a losing battle. Bracing himself on the driver's side door, he kicked at the passenger side window hard as he could.

"AAAHHHH!" Alex's veins bulged at the strength of his kicks. The window finally smashed out. Rain rushed in as Alex climbed out. Water pelted his face as he climbed onto the roof of the car. He could hardly see through the rain. He looked at the lights of the truck, trying to see who was driving. Through the heavy rain, he could see a man with blonde hair driving the truck.

"Oh, god." Fear consumed Alex. Glowing red eyes looked back at him. Another person possessed by the Awari. He put the truck in reverse again, then drove towards Alex at full speed. Alex jumped off the roof of the car to the side of the road. He watched in horror as the truck plowed into the car. It smashed it into the rail with such force that every window on the car blew out. Alex was soaking wet lying on the ground. Red and blue flashing lights came out of nowhere. A cop car slid to a stop with its sirens blazing. The cop jumped out of the car, gun drawn. He looked at Alex getting soaked on the ground.

"What the fuck is going on?" he yelled over the loud rain to Alex. Alex had no words. He didn't fully understand what was going on himself, how could he describe it to the cop? The truck went in reverse again, then drove directly towards them. The truck hit the cop and kept reversing towards Alex. The cop's body flew and landed on the hood of Alex's car. He could see blood coming out of the cop's mouth. His eyes were wide open and lifeless.

"OH SHIT!" Alex screamed and scrambled to get out of the way of the murderous truck. He narrowly missed being hit by the truck, and landed on his butt on the wet street. He lay on the ground in shock. The rain was assaulting him more and more by the minute. He felt a fire start to burn in his stomach. He jumped up and looked directly at the driver in the truck. He smiled at Alex and turned on his high beams. Alex shielded his eyes from the light. He could hear the gears grinding on the truck as it moved forward towards him.

Alex was no longer scared. Anger boiled inside of him. He was angry about being chased out of his own home. He was angry that he was standing in the rain facing this thing he had no idea about. Alex could feel his jaw clench and his hands form into fists. The truck was headed for him. Thoughts of Daniel moved in and out of his mind. He thought of their trips together and thought about how they would never happen again. He thought about how fucked up things had become because of a trinket they bought. He missed Daniel so much. He could think and reminisce about him all day. But right now, he had to find a way to stop this creature.

The truck was almost upon him, but he didn't care. Something in him started to build. He felt hot as if his soul were stoking a fire. He looked at his arms and noticed that the rain hitting his skin was steaming and sizzling. His vision drastically changed. He could not only see the truck, but he could see the energy from that thing inside of it. He saw the creatures' heart, as if he was looking through an x-ray machine. At that moment, he felt peace for a split second and closed his eyes. The truck was only moments from running him down. He opened his eyes and saw symbols swirling around the truck. They formed into one image directly over the murderous truck. Alex instinctively put his hand out towards the truck. It instantly exploded. Pieces of the truck flew around him, but none touched him. The creature inside hit the ground and landed directly in front of Alex. Its right arm was torn off. Alex looked directly at the creature. His head was twisted all the way around. His neck was twisted and broken. He opened his mouth, and that same dark voice rumbled from within him.

"I see you discovered the powers the Awari awakens inside of you. We need to be extra cautious with you from this point."

Alex looked down at his hands. They were glowing a faint red. He had abilities. He could feel his blood coursing through his body. He could feel every organ and every movement of his muscles. He couldn't believe what he'd just done.

Blood shot from the creatures' mouth as he continued to speak.

"Your aura smells so good. Different than the others. I wish I could have tasted it."

Alex felt the urge to stomp on the thing's head, but he stopped himself. He needed to hear more.

"You're learning fast. I should have focused only on you and not given you time to regroup. I needed that fear you had. It feeds us and keeps your powers from working." Alex listened intently at the twisted head. If he was afraid, he was defenseless. That's how they managed to steal souls from people at the peak of their fear. Alex was learning something new every minute. The Awari held so many secrets. Alex debated on whether to try to kill this creature or not. He seemed harmless now that he was disfigured, but Alex wasn't sure if it would die. He couldn't leave it out here to attack another person.

"You may have awakened your powers, but we still have your Daniel," the creature laughed maniacally. Alex's anger surged as he jumped up and slammed his boots onto the creature's face.

Alex needed to find out who else had touched this Awari. He felt deep down that it was his job to keep them alive long enough to send these creatures back to hell. He needed to get to Jared now.

He ran as fast as he could to the next block. The rain had let up just a little, making it less of a hassle to run without slipping. He hailed a cab and jumped in. He watched police cars head in the direction he'd just come from. The cab driver turned around to Alex and smiled.

"Did you hear what just happened around the block?" Alex shook his head no. The cab driver took a drag of his cigarette and turned up what Alex thought was the radio.

"A cop just got killed around the corner. Crazy, right?" The cabbie was listening to a police scanner. He turned the windshield wipers on. The cabbie started talking to Alex about his childhood, when a woman's voice came on the radio.

55

"We are searching for a white male about six feet two with black hair and...," Alex turned pale as he listened to the rest of the description. *Oh shit! They are looking for me!* Alex thought to himself. The cabbie slammed on the brakes and put a beer Alex didn't know he had been holding, in the cup holder. He stuck his hand out towards Alex.

"Twelve dollars and fifteen cents please," he said. Alex gave him a twenty and told him to keep the change. He stepped out into the rain and looked up at the swanky condominiums Jared lived in.

Chapter 5

Alex walked into the lobby and stopped in his tracks. He noticed the security guard standing next to the elevator had blood red eyes. "Fuck," he said under his breath in frustration. *Where the hell are they all coming from?* He was so confused. It seemed like everywhere he turned he ran into another creature. He thought about yelling for the other security guards, but stopped himself. They hadn't noticed anything wrong with the guard by the elevator. Alex realized he' was able to see them while others couldn't. Touching the Awari had changed not only his aura but also his body. It gave those creatures the ability to see him, but it also gave him the ability to see them. A searing pain started shooting through his arm. He closed his mouth shut tight so he wouldn't scream out. Those weird symbols that he'd seen on the creatures, started pushing up through the skin on his arm. Panicking, he ran into the corner of the lobby and sat in a chair facing the street. It felt as if someone were pouring boiling water onto his arm. The symbols glowed red and broke through his skin. He started sweating, and his arm went limp. The symbols settled on his arm and started forming around it like a sleeve. He looked at his arm, now stained with a tattoo of symbols. It glowed bright red, then eventually settled into black. Every few seconds he could see a glowing red light tracing the black lines.

Alex believed that the more he was around those creatures, the more he would start to change. He could feel the burning inside growing. He knew he needed to get to Jared now. He took a breath and stood up. He started to walk towards the elevator. He took a few steps, then the whole building shook.

"WHOA!" Alex fell sideways. It felt like an explosion had happened above him. He heard screams and looked outside. He saw rubble and dust falling outside the lobby window from the floors above. Somehow, he could sense that Jared was in danger. It was freaking him out. He hadn't seen Jared in so long, but he just knew that Jared needed him. Or maybe he needed Jared. A fear crept into Alex's heart. It was strange because it didn't belong to him. It was Jared's. Alex felt him from upstairs. Jared was changing. Alex felt it deep in his bones. He had somehow formed a link to him. He must be close. Alex grabbed his arm and stood tall. The pain was unbearable, but he didn't have much time. He mustered up all the courage he had and turned the corner to the elevator bank. People had been screaming and running throughout the lobby since the explosion, but not the security guard. He was standing in front of the elevator grinning. Alex felt like those red eyes were burning into his soul.

The guard opened his mouth and small puffs of smoke came out as he spoke. "I see you have some power too," he said looking at his newly tattooed arm. Alex didn't say anything. If he'd learned anything, it was that these things loved to talk. The more they talked, the more he was learning about the Awari. The guard turned his head slightly to the left. Smoke came pouring from his nose and eyes like an angry bull. He moved slowly towards Alex, taking small casual steps.

"You'll find out I'm a little more difficult to get away from than the others. I am one of the older ones. Some of us have talents the others do not." Alex digested that information for later. He tried to call upon the anger he'd felt earlier so he could use his new powers. He couldn't focus enough, the pain in his arm was extreme. He tried to elevate his breathing and closed his eyes. Alex opened his eyes and jumped back in surprise.

"What the fuck!" The guard was standing right in front of him. He grabbed Alex's arm and threw him to the ground like he weighed nothing. *How the fuck did he get in front of me so fast?* Alex wondered, trying to get away from the guard. He was trying so hard to comprehend everything. The guard stood above Alex.

"This smoke distorts the senses. What may have seemed like a second to you, was really a minute. Are you having problems standing up?" The guard started laughing.

Alex got dizzy as soon as the guard asked that question. His vision swayed every time he tried to stand up. A shockwave of pain came from Alex's stomach.

"AAAHHH!" The guard had kicked him in the stomach, forcing him to fall back onto the floor. Alex heard voices coming from the direction of the lobby. People were yelling for the guard to stop beating him up.

"SHUT THE FUCK UP!" The guard's rumbling voice shook the lobby walls. Alex looked up at him as smoke poured from his eyes. He turned his attention to the people in the lobby and started blowing smoke towards them. One by one, people started to drop to the ground and pass out. Alex wrapped his good arm around his stomach and crawled around the corner towards a chair. He tried to call out to Jared in his mind. The smoke was everywhere now. A man in a blue blazer and khaki pants started running towards them, holding his arm to his face. He started coughing as he got closer to the guard.

"What are you doing? Stop and figure out where all this damned smoke is coming from right now, or you're fired!" The man must have been the property manager.

"Okay. I'll take care of it personally," the creature smiled wickedly. He started walking towards the property manager. Without hesitation, he picked the man up by one leg and threw him through the window of the lobby.

"OH MY GOD!" Alex screamed out in horrified disbelief. The man landed on the sidewalk outside with a loud thud. He did not get up. A large piece of glass was sticking out of his neck. The creature just stood there looking at the man he'd just murdered. No remorse or guilt on his face. He actually looked satisfied with himself. That was all the distraction Alex needed to escape. He jumped up and ran as fast as he could to look for the stairs of the building. *No way am I waiting for a fucking elevator with that thing chasing me*, Alex thought as he ran. He was grateful the pain in his arm was starting to subside. There was still a lot of commotion coming from the lobby area. He tried to block it out and focus on finding Jared.

Alex felt a sensation in his eyes. Suddenly he saw the building as if it were a blueprint. He knew exactly where the stairs were located. He turned around and saw the creature pick up a large vase. Alex could sense the change in the building. Something as small as a vase being moved shifted the blueprints in his eyes. The guard lifted the vase and aimed it at Alex. Alex ran and ducked his head as the vase came flying towards him. He made his way to the door of the stairs as the vase shattered behind him. He could hear the creature chasing him, his steps shaking the floor. Alex opened the stairway door and closed it behind him. His adrenaline was pumping at an all-time high. He turned his focus to the door. He felt the heat inside of him, just like the last time he'd used his powers. He watched in fascination as the metal doorknob started dripping and melting into the door frame. He turned around and ran as fast as he could up the steps.

He could hear the creature below trying to get the door open. Alex was running so fast that he nearly fell up the steps. He could sense that Jared was close when he landed on the tenth floor. He opened the stairway door and ran down the hall. He knocked on the door harder than he should have. He could feel Jared on the other side of the door.

"Jared!", Alex yelled banging on the door.

"It's Alex! You have something I need. Please open the door. We need to talk." Alex could hear the door to the stairway open down the hall.

"Jared please open the door! I know how you feel. I'm going through the same changes. That idol did something to us, and now I have these creatures chasing me. They're trying to kill me!" Alex turned around to see the shape of the guard at the end of the hallway. His panic level was rising.

"PLEASE OPEN THE DOOR!" He banged on the door repeatedly. Alex wouldn't stop banging on the door. He turned and saw the creature moving slowly towards him out of the corner of his eyes. It was laughing as it came towards him. Alex didn't have enough time to focus before his vision got blurry. But through the haze, he could see the top half of the creature turn to smoke while the legs remained flesh. Alex blinked in disbelief as he watched the guard run towards him. The door to Jared's apartment suddenly opened and Jared stepped out. Alex looked at his face. Jared seemed like he was in a trance. His eyes glowed blue.

Chapter 6

Jared had once again let Chris drag him out to a club. He hated clubs. His affluent upbringing had made it easy for him to get into the most upscale and elite clubs since he was fourteen. Now they held no real appeal to him. His parents never understood why he never took to their lavish lifestyle the way they had. They had inherited a large sum of money before Jared was born. By the time he was old enough to walk, his parents were going to any and every party they could. They left it up to Ann, the woman who ran their house, to raise him. They loved to brag and show off their wealth. Jared couldn't have felt more different than them. His parents spoiled him with money, but never attention or affection. He attended the best schools and dined at the most revered restaurants around the globe. But Jared would have preferred homecooked meals with his parents. Jared vaguely remembered all the places they'd travelled to growing up, but one place never left his mind. When he was around five years old, his parents took him on one of their many trips to Paris. They dropped him off at different tourist attractions and left him to his own devices. One day, they dropped Jared off at a museum of art. Jared would sit in the museum and just stare at the art for hours. His inquisitive mind wanted to know everything about the art. From its origins to how it was made. Jared realized he had a deep love for art. While his parents were concerned about the latest fashions, he was researching details about specific paintings. Art had such a profound impact on his life, that he decided to become an art dealer. Art inspired him to be himself and not be afraid to stand out.

Jared had dark brown hair growing up and always hated it. When he decided to bleach his hair white, he took pride in the fact that he looked completely different than everyone he knew. He was now a work of art. Jared discovered he was gay around the age of ten. He realized this when he was only attracted to the male curators at the museums he would visit. His parents either knew or just didn't care. They didn't blink an eye the first time he brought a boy home after a date. Being immersed in the art world, Jared met people from all walks of life.

The day he met Alex and Daniel, Jared had just finished purchasing a piece he'd been searching for since the year before. Chris made the introductions and they all greeted each other pleasantly. Jared could feel there was chemistry between Alex and Daniel, but couldn't tell what their deal was. They weren't overtly affectionate, but he could tell they were together. Jared thought Alex was sexy as hell. He had thick, dark hair and eyebrows. His whole demeanor was very outgoing and jovial. He seemed very comfortable in his own skin. Daniel was the exact opposite. He was quiet and barely interacted when they made conversation. After his initial attraction to Alex, Jared realized he liked him as a person as well. They talked a lot during the art show and exchanged numbers. They didn't keep in touch after that, though.

The only other time Jared saw Alex was at his yard sale. Chris told him about what happened to Daniel and how Alex was selling his things. Jared thought that was tragic for him. He caught a glimpse of Alex's grieving silhouette walking around the yard sale that day. Jared could feel the sadness coming from Alex and didn't know what to say to him. He decided to leave him alone with his grief. Jared was about to tell Chris he was ready to go, when he spotted a small statue. It was unlike anything he'd ever encountered at a museum or art gallery. The markings on it looked tribal. Jared was instantly intrigued.

He told Chris to settle up with Alex for him, and grabbed the statue. It was warm in his hands. He figured it had been sitting in the sun all day, so naturally it would be warm to the touch. He put the statue in his glove compartment and made his way home. For the next few days, Jared studied the statue and tried to see if he could figure out its origin. He was in the middle of reading an article about ancient idols when Chris texted him. He wanted to go out that night. Jared would much rather read the article, but he gave in to Chris. On the way to the club, Jared started getting anxious. It was a weird sensation that seemed to come out of nowhere. He walked straight into the club without waiting because he knew the owners. He spotted Chris at the bar. They ordered drinks, but Jared's mind was on the little statue at home.

"I think that guy is checking you out," Chris yelled to him over the loud music. Jared looked at the guy across the room staring at him. His eyes looked red. Jared looked into his drink, thinking it was stronger than he thought.

"I'll be back," Jared put his drink down and made his way to the bathroom. He was dizzy all of a sudden. He turned the cold water on and splashed some on his face. His skin felt hot. He looked at himself in the mirror as a chunk of his white hair fell into his eyes.

"Chris spiked my drink," he said to his reflection. That was the only explanation he could think of that would explain his sudden dizziness and nausea. The bathroom door opened to his right, but he didn't pay it any attention.

"Your aura smells fresh. You just touched it didn't you?" A deep, foreboding voice echoed throughout the bathroom.

"What? What the hell are you talking about?" Jared turned towards the man who had come into the bathroom. He was standing at the door with his head tilted. He was thin and dressed all in black. His long black hair fell down his back. He had the palest skin Jared had ever seen. Jared watched as the guy's eyes looked him up and down in appraisal. His eyes were glowing red.

"Shit! Are…are you okay man? Your eyes are…" before Jared could finish his sentence, the man rushed towards him. His hands went around Jared's throat, lifting him off his feet, and slamming him into the mirror. Glass shattered and fell around them. Jared's dizzy spell vanished. Shock and fear overcame him. The glowing red eyes grew brighter and brighter as the hands around his throat tightened. It

66

took Jared a few seconds to react to the sudden burst of violence. He wrapped his hands around the deranged man's wrists and tried to peel them off his neck.

"Your fear is intoxicating!" Jared struggled for air as he moved his leg underneath his attacker. His vision got blurry. He knew soon he would pass out.

"Let me go!" Jared choked out and shoved his knee into his attacker's groin.

"AAAAHHH!" His attacker screamed and let go of his neck. Jared inhaled loudly, trying to get oxygen. Before he could fully catch his breath, his attacker grabbed him by both arms and threw him across the bathroom. Jared was air bound for what seemed like forever before crashing into the bathroom door.

"FUCK THIS!" Jared yelled and got to his feet. He frantically grabbed at the door handle, and ran out back into the club.

Jared's body was vibrating with adrenaline. He searched the club for Chris, but his eyes landed on another strange looking guy with red eyes.

"What the hell is happening?" Jared asked himself in fear. He was standing on the dance floor now, head swiveling from left to right. People were staring at him and pointing.

"Look at his eyes," a young guy said pointing directly at him. Jared looked at the mirror behind the bar and realized his eyes were glowing too. They were a brilliant blue. Shock made him stumble backwards. Something was wrong. This had to be a bad dream. He shook his head trying to clear it and looked for Chris. His eyes landed on the man from the bathroom. His red eyes burned into Jared's. Jared turned around to run and was stopped by the other strange guy he'd seen with red eyes. He was surrounded. Jared panicked and tried to think of an escape. His mind still couldn't make sense of what was happening. *Where's Chris?* Jared asked himself, trying to formulate a plan of attack.

"Ouch!" A burning sensation slid down Jared's arms and down to his fingertips. He looked down at his fingers as his vision got blurry again. Jared blinked in surprise, then his vision split. It was like his eyes had split into small squares.

"What in the actual hell?" What looked like blocks of symbols appeared in front of him. His fingers twitched as he thought about escaping. As if the blocks of symbols heard him, they started to form into a shield around Jared. The two guys with red eyes looked hesitant after seeing the blocks form, but they still moved closer to Jared. The club goers were totally unaware of everything going on. Jared guessed that he was hallucinating all of this. His theory that his drink had been spiked was starting to ring more and more true. Jared's fingertips moved, and the blocks started to direct themselves towards the guys with the red eyes. It felt natural for them to form. It felt as if the blocks were reacting on their own, protecting him. A feeling of defense overcame Jared and somehow he understood the feeling belonged to the blocks. It felt like how a pet would protect their owner. Jared's fear started to go away as he realized he was in no danger, but the creatures with red eyes were. He spread his arms wide, one arm towards each creature. He wanted to hit them with the blocks. The blocks shot out from his hands and hit each creature square in their chests.

"OH SHIT!" Jared looked at his fingertips in wonder as both creatures fell to the floor. Jared looked around, and still no one was looking in their direction. The music was loud, people danced and drank all around him. Chris was nowhere to be found. Jared's heart started pounding loudly in his ears. *I have to get out of here*, Jared told himself and made a beeline for the exit of the club.

Getting to his car, driving home, and entering his condo was a blur. Jared's fingers shook uncontrollably as he locked his door. Jared still felt like he was under the influence of some sort of drug. He thought there was no way anything he'd just gone through had been real. He fell asleep minutes later, not even remembering if he made it into the bedroom or not. That night as he slept, symbols invaded his dreams. Symbols he couldn't decipher but seemed familiar to him. When Jared got up the next day, he instinctively looked at his hands. He blinked twice and came to the shocking conclusion that last night had been real. Blocks of symbols formed in front of his face. He didn't know whether he should scream, cry, or be intrigued. What he did know was something unnatural was happening. He got dressed and prepared to go to the main library to do some research. The symbols invaded his eyesight again, making it hard for him to concentrate.

"I can't see!" Jared screamed inside his empty condo. His fear rose. He sat down on the floor and tried to concentrate on the symbols. He needed to know how to control them and why they appeared out of nowhere. No matter how hard he tried that day, he couldn't control the symbols like he had at the club the night before. Jared decided he would not leave his condo until he figured out what was going on. He needed to learn how to control this newfound power he had. His phone dinged multiple times a day from calls and texts from concerned friends. He couldn't respond to them without sounding crazy.

Jared didn't know how long he stayed couped up in his apartment practicing making the blocks appear and disappear. Time didn't matter. He was getting better and better at his control. At one point, Jared realized he could make the blocks do different things and make them form into different shapes. It started to feel as natural as breathing to Jared to command the blocks. He had been in the middle of creating a block that could cause an explosion when an overwhelming feeling of despair flooded him. He lost his concentration and the block hit one of the walls in his condo. The wall shook as the blocks exploded.

"Dammit!" Jared ran over to his window and watched debris fall to the ground below. That feeling of despair overcame him again and then turned into fear.

Something wasn't right. There was something evil near him. He could feel it. He stood at his door and commanded a shield of blocks in front of him. He felt his vision changing as the blocks consumed his sight.

"Jared!" A frantic voice yelled from behind his front door. Whoever it was, was banging on the door like the police. Jared looked through the peephole and recognized Alex immediately. He looked scared and kept looking over his shoulder. *What the hell is he doing here?* Jared thought in confusion. The feeling that he was in danger became unbearable.

"It's Alex! You have something I need. Please open the door. We need to talk." Alex's voice rose an octave. He hadn't seen Alex since the yard sale.

"Jared, please open the door! I know how you feel. I'm going through the same changes. That idol did something to us and now I have these creatures chasing me. They're trying to kill me!" So many questions raced through Jared's mind. Alex was going through changes, too? What idol? Creatures? Was Alex seeing those creatures too? How?

"PLEASE OPEN THE DOOR!" Alex's voice was now a scream. Jared took a deep breath and pulled on his doorknob.

Chapter 7

Alex hadn't seen Jared in such a long time. He'd forgotten how angular his face was.

He had a goatee that Alex did not remember him having when they'd first met. The

same tattooed symbols that were burning Alex's arms appeared around Jared's eyes.

Dark circles rimmed his glowing eyes. Jared stepped in front of Alex. He didn't say a

word. Alex could see what seemed like small square structures forming in front of

Jared. They started to form around the both of them. He knew Jared was making this

happen. The legs of the creature stopped moving and the top half of the creature started

to reform.

"Jared," the creature's seductive voice filled the hallway.

"You finally decided to come out and play." Jared stayed silent. His eyes

glowed bright blue now. The creature picked up a large table in the hallway and threw

it at them. The square that had been floating in front of them reacted instantly to form a

wall. The table smashed into the wall and broke apart into pieces. The creature yelled

in frustration. The square reformed and started floating in front of them and then the

wall was gone. Alex thought maybe Jared was exerting too much energy. He thought

maybe he could somehow combine his newfound powers with Jared's. He tried to

focus his power, but his arm started burning again. The pain was almost unbearable.

Alex dropped to the floor. Jared looked down at him with those strange glowing blue

eyes. His white hair partly covered his right eye. His black leather jacket fit tight around his lean body. Jared was dressed in goth clothing with black leather boots that went up to his knees. He had thin chains that went from the front of his belt loop to the back of his belt. He was wearing black leather gloves with the fingertips cut out. Alex thought he looked badass.

The creature laughed. A huge cloud of black smoke poured from his mouth and eyes. The smoke billowed towards them.

Oh shit! What the fuck do we do now? Alex thought, partially bent over in pain. The floating squares in front of them started to vibrate. The cloud of smoke was getting closer. Alex yelled, "Don't breathe it in! It affects your senses." Jared shook his head in understanding then looked straight ahead. The squares started to shift and spin. They started to spin so fast that Alex could no longer see them. The squares behind them also started to spin. Pictures on the hallway walls were blown off. The smoke was caught up in the wind Jared's squares were creating and was being pushed back. All that remained was the creature in smoke form. The squares suddenly stopped spinning. The squares behind them shot forward and circled around the cloud of smoke that was the creature. They spun faster and faster around the smoke, locking it in one place. Alex could see the legs of the creature trying to form again, but the force of the wind swirling around it made it almost impossible. Jared's eyes grew brighter and brighter. Alex watched in disbelief and awe. The squares suddenly stopped spinning. The wind stopped and the squares disappeared. The legs of the creature started to form and then the torso and then the head. Jared had forced the creature back into human form.

"Why Jared, who knew a pussy boy like you had it in you?" The creature laughed hard. Alex noticed the squares were slowly forming again behind the creature. Their shape changed into what appeared to be hundreds of arrow heads. The creature continued laughing, unaware. It opened its mouth to speak at the very moment hundreds of squares in arrow form shot through its neck. Arrows came from all directions. The creature was still talking as his head fell from his body. Jared looked down at the severed head.

"Fuck you."

Without speaking, they walked into Jared's condo. Alex could hear the traffic below clearly because a wall in Jared's condo was blown out. He remembered seeing rubble fall to the street below as he was being attacked by that creature in the lobby. He looked around the condo awkwardly. Alex figured they had a few minutes before the police or some other form of authority arrived.

"Jared, where is the idol?" Alex cut right to the chase. He came there for one thing, and one thing only. Jared's eyes pulsed blue as he pointed to the table next to the sofa. Alex had almost forgotten what the idol looked like. *All of this destruction and drama for this tourist trinket?* Alex thought sadly. The Awari was turquoise with traces of gold around it. It appeared to be a head sitting on two legs and two large disks on the sides of its head. Alex reached for the idol and his arm exploded in pain. He immediately felt dizzy. He could see that flames were rising from his arms, but he was not being burned. All the pain seemed to come from within. He could once again feel something building within himself. Alex's vision started to change.

"Hey, you okay, Alex?" Alex heard Jared's concerned voice, but he couldn't respond. He felt frozen in place. Flashes of images started to appear in front of his eyes. He looked at a large mirror hanging on Jared's wall. His eyes were glowing bright white. A sense of fear overcame him and then it was gone. Alex felt like he was having an out of body experience. Physically he was in Jared's condo, but mentally he knew he was somewhere else.

74

Images of a temple started to appear into his mind. He was no longer inside his body. Alex's subconscious was inside of someone else. A man he'd never seen before. Surprisingly, that didn't scare him.

Alex was now inside a temple. His chest was bare as he looked around at the structure. He appeared to be a warrior. He stood over six feet tall. His dark hair complimented his dark skin. He had large, gold arm bracers on. From his waist down, he had on yellow and red garb. His lean body slinked through the temple as if he was afraid to be seen. The temple was dark, only lit with torches. Alex could hear screams coming from the darkened hallway in front of him. Alex could hear the heartbeat of the man whose body he was inside. It was thunderous. Whatever was happening, he was afraid. Snakes slithered past him, but he never stopped or looked down at them. A very large set of stairs were in front of him. He held on to the side of the wall and slowly walked towards the direction of the screams. The smell of something rotten attacked his senses. Each step he took made his heart beat harder and harder. The anticipation of what he would find was killing him. The sweat from his brow dripped into his eyes as he crept further and further down the darkened stairs. He reached the bottom of the steps and paused. The torches made his shadow appear large on the ground. He stopped and tried to figure out what to do next. Alex could feel that the man had a deep fear of what he might see. Anxiety was running through his blood. He peered around the corner and found himself viewing some sort of ceremony.

There was a large circle drawn into the dirt in the middle of the torch lit room. A large wall encircled the room. Horror filled him as he realized people were tied to every inch of the wall. Some of the people tied to the wall were dead. Others, alive, appeared to have been hanging there for days, even weeks, from the looks of their flesh. Alex heard the voice of the man he was inside. He whispered the name Itzel. He'd whispered it as a plea. Alex felt a deep affection at the mention of that name. It was someone the man loved. He was looking for her. Alex felt the man's emotions deep in his heart as if they were his. His eyes searched fearfully for her among the bodies. He found her. His breath caught in his throat at the sight of her. She was beautiful. She was tall, with a long delicate neck. She had thick, long, dark hair. Her scared grey eyes caught his. She was dressed in all white and exuded a natural elegance that had drawn the warrior to her the first time they'd met. Alex could feel the love the man had for this woman. A feeling that this was his wife overwhelmed him. The love felt like the love Alex had for Daniel. He could see that she was tied to the wall along with her entire village. They all had blood smeared on their faces and ropes around their necks. His wife screamed out his name in fear and desperation. She screamed, "Acan!" over and over. *Acan*. That's what the man that Alex was inside was named. Acan almost cried at the sight of his wife hanging from that wall. Another man walked from behind one of the walls and put the idol on a tablet facing them.

Alex felt a deep burning hate inside of Acan's body towards the man. And intense fear. A familial bond was strong between them. This was Acan's father. He stood tall and taut with authority. He was huge and menacing. He was as tall as Acan with long white hair. His dark eyes looked soulless. Acan's heart almost stopped. His father was very powerful and Acan knew he was no match for him.

Alex, now Acan, noticed the Idol was connected to another identical idol. They were connected like conjoined twins. His father turned in his direction, he knew Acan was there. *Isic*. The name floated through Alex's head. That was Acan's father's name. His eyes glowed a bright red. His voice almost a growl. Acan could hear Isic's words in his head even though his mouth wasn't moving. The people on the wall started to scream. Their screams were soul piercing. Acan couldn't take anymore. His fear for Itzel gave him courage he did not have. He raced towards that tablet as Isic spoke louder and louder.

The idol on the tablet glowed. Acan stopped in his tracks. He could see those creatures racing into the room. They stopped and stood at the entrances of the room. His father's army had arrived. Isic's evil eyes glowed red as he pulled out a sickle hook. He swung for Acan's head. Acan ducked, barely missing a beheading, and reached for the bow and arrow on his back. Itzel had a look of terror on her face. Isic smiled in pleasure and ran at Acan. He was going to kill them. Acan swallowed his fear and looked at Itzel's scared face. He had to save her. The creatures stood watching and not moving. The idol glowed brighter and brighter. Symbols flashed under it. Isic was so fast. Acan did not see Isic as he moved towards him. The sickle hit Acan's arm brace full force. Acan jumped back and tried his best to get a good aim on his father with his arrow. He was afraid he would miss and hit one of the people hanging on the wall. Or worse, hit Itzel. He thought quickly to reach for his knife. He tossed his bow and arrow aside. The people on the wall started screaming again as the idol glowed. Acan could see that people on the wall were starting to die. His fear for Itzel intensified. He didn't look at her. He wouldn't be able to concentrate on saving her if he did. White shadows were being pulled from the people hanging from the wall and into the idol. Acan's wife yelled his name frantically and pulled at her restraints. Isic stopped and looked at Acan, then at Itzel with a sinister smile. He knew Acan was here for her. Acan yelled her name in fear.

"ITZEL!" Isic started to run towards her with the sickle in front of him.

He was aiming to ram the sickle right inside of her. Acan didn't know if he was fast enough to stop him. Fear pushed him to move faster than he'd ever moved before. Itzel cried out Acan's name as he ran towards her. Isic's laughter echoed throughout the temple as if it were coming straight from hell. Her beautiful gray eyes were now filled with terror. Acan ran faster, hoping he would reach the bow and arrow in time. He knew he only had one shot. The idol glowed brighter and brighter as the people hanging on the walls started screaming again. It was a strange sound, almost like painful pleasure. The white shadows floated past and through Acan, making him feel violated. He could feel their dreams and desires as they moved through him. It was almost as if he could touch them.

"That thing is sucking out their souls," Acan said out loud in shock. Acan thought of how many souls this thing may have collected already and felt sick. The ground started to shake. Isic was almost upon Itzel. The ground was shaking harder and harder. Acan took aim. He prayed to the gods that he would hit his mark. He pulled the bow back and shot the arrow as Isic lunged for Itzel with the sickle in his hand.

"ALEX! ARE YOU IN THERE?" The images started to fade. Jared was shaking Alex roughly back and forth. He tried as hard as he could to bring the image back, but it was fading more and more.

"I need to know if I saved her!" Alex cried shaking the dizziness off. The temple was gone. So was Acan, Itzel, and that lunatic Isic. Alex was back inside his own body, back inside Jared's condo.

"How will I know if I saved her?" Alex started to cry and fell back onto Jared's sofa.

"Save who? What just happened? You were frozen like you were in a trance." Alex heard Jared talking, but he couldn't concentrate. What he'd just experienced had been so real. He could feel himself shaking from the emotional toll it had taken on his body. Alex was drained. Tears fell down his face as he thought of the woman that was once his wife. He put his hands to his face.

"Did I save her?" He felt a warm hand on his shoulder. He put his hands down and looked at Jared. His eyes were glowing, but they were a lighter shade of blue. He sat down next to Alex. He started to speak and then hesitated.

78

"What is it, Jared?" He was confused as to why Jared seemed troubled.

"You didn't save her, Alex., Jared said as Alex's eyes went wide.

"How do you know that?" Alex asked. Jared narrowed his eyes like he didn't know how to say what he was about to say.

"I don't know, I just feel it. These symbols communicate with me. They are telling me they can show me what you were seeing. It doesn't feel like it was a good outcome. I can't explain it, but I can show you how whatever you just saw ended. If you want, that is." Jared was talking in a soft tone. Alex needed to know. He was afraid to see, but he had to know. He nodded his head for Jared to show him.

Jared's eyes glowed light blue. He looked straight ahead. One square started slowly forming in front of them. The square pulsed a light blue, then white, and then light blue again. Alex could feel himself starting to calm down. He felt like he was being lulled into a trance again. Jared's eyes flashed bright and the square expanded to the width of the room. A vision started to appear on the square. It was operating like a projector. Alex felt like he was about to watch a movie. He could not make out what he was seeing at first. Colors and symbols were flashing across the square. He blinked a few times and then he saw clearly. He was seeing the temple, but it wasn't from Acan's perspective. Alex was seeing it from the view of Itzel. Itzel's eyes landed on Isic's crazed form in front of her. She could see Acan out of the corner of her eyes. They both watched Isic start reciting some sort of incantation. Then Isic started running towards her. Alex could now feel her fear just as strongly as he'd felt Acan's. His breath left his body at the terror seizing him. Itzel watched Acan holding his bow. Itzel saw how much Acan was shaking. She could see the look of fear on Acan's face. She watched the arrow release from the bow. Itzel closed her eyes and held her breath. When her eyes opened, she was looking down at her stomach. The sickle hook had been plunged into her. The pain and shock were so great that she became numb. Isic

79

had a smile on his face as he continued to say the incantation. Itzel's half dead gaze landed on Acan. He was horrified at the sight of the sickle in his wife's stomach. Tears streamed down his face. Alex could see Itzel's restrained hands trying to reach out to Acan, to him. She looked up in a daze. The creatures who had remained still were now starting to come into the temple. Acan stood up and screamed out Itzel's name.

His voice was laced with anguish. He could see Itzel was fading away. The creatures now surrounded the circle. Acan's tear-soaked face looked around frantically trying to figure out what to do. His eyes landed on the idol. The Awari. All of this mayhem was because of that idol. Acan stood up and started to run for it. A knife sliced through the air and went through his leg. Acan screamed in pain and his steps faltered. He was bleeding, but dragged himself towards the Awari. He had to destroy it for what it had done to Itzel. To everyone in the temple. Isic moved slowly towards Acan. Like a predator hunting its' prey. The creatures moved in closer to Acan with knives drawn. Acan could see a view of Itzel's stomach again, blood streaming out of it. The vision on the square in Jared's living room started flickering. Alex prayed the vision would hold. He held his breath as he watched Acan reach for the Awari. Isic was right behind him. Another knife appeared out of nowhere and went into Acan's back. Acan whimpered in pain and fell to the temple floor. Isic laughed and started to step back. Acan started crawling, leaving a blood trail behind him. Suddenly everything went quiet in the temple. His father looked back at Itzel with a scared look on his face. Acan's body started to glow white. There was no sound. The sound was being sucked out of the temple room. Energy was being generated from Acan and growing in force.

"Oh shit!" Alex screamed in amazement at the light coming from Acan's body and beaming into Jared's square. Cracks started to appear in the floor of the temple as Acan glowed brighter and brighter. The creatures started to move back from

80

Acan as rings of light started to pulse from him. The creatures stepped further back in confusion. Acan reached up and grabbed the Awari. He seemed like he looked directly at Alex and Jared, then at Itzel. Alex could see his lips moving, but again there was no sound. Isic's mouth fell open in surprise at what he'd just seen, and he started to run.

Acan closed his eyes as light exploded from his body. Alex could see Isic catch fire as he tried to run. He ran down the hall screaming. All at once his creatures began to burn. The room shook and swayed. Small traces of light from the torches were being pulled into Acan. He sat motionless for a minute. He looked up at Itzel. All was calm at first. Then all at once, there was an explosion of light and fire. The light flew throughout the temple, burning everything in its path. Through the light and fire, Alex could see Acan, but then everything turned black. The images on Jared's square disappeared. Alex watched the square reduce in size and slowly fade away.

Alex could feel himself starting to fall apart inside. His shoulders started to shake from his cries. Jared pulled him into a light hug as he cried. Alex felt pain and loss deep in his soul. Pain for Acan, pain for Itzel, pain for Daniel.

Alex wiped his face and tried to stand up. He stumbled backwards, almost falling over. Jared caught him by the wrist.

"Whoa, easy there. Just sit down and try to get your bearings. That was a lot to take in. For me too." Jared sighed and helped Alex sit back down. His eyes were no longer glowing when he looked down at Alex. Alex gasped in shock.

"What?" Jared looked around in confusion after Alex gasped.

"Your eyes," Alex pointed to Jared. Jared's once dark brown eyes were now a stunning gray. Just like Itzel's. Alex felt like he was looking into her eyes.

"I have to show you something," Jared pulled his shirt up. A very large scar was on his stomach.

"The scar appeared after I touched the idol. Now I know where it's from. It's Itzel's scar."

Alex stared in shock. He stood up and looked in the mirror on Jared's wall to see if his suspicions were true. Sure enough, his eyes had changed colors as well. Now they were dark brown. Like Acan.

"I think I'm starting to understand what's happening." Alex said looking at his new eyes. A loud banging on the door made them both jump in fright. A loud voice yelled out, "Police! Open up right now!"

Chapter 8

"I don't suppose one of your newfound powers is flight?" Alex asked only half joking. Jared looked at him with amusement.

"Uh, no." The banging and yelling continued.

"Open up this door, or we will break it in!" Jared grabbed Alex's arm and pulled him down the hall towards the bedrooms. Alex looked back to the living room as Jared rushed them into his bedroom. He could hear the front door being kicked in. The sound of multiple people running into the condo filled the air. Jared whispered to Alex to back up to the corner.

They were standing close to each other with their backs to the wall.

"What are we going to do? We can't use our powers. I don't want to hurt them." Alex whispered in a panic. He looked at Jared, whose eyes were now glowing a bright blue.

"We won't," Jared whispered calmly. Alex saw squares forming in front of them. They started changing from blue to white. They surrounded them and formed an invisible wall in front of them.

"Don't worry. They can't see us." Jared whispered to Alex. Alex had been close to having a panic attack at that point. Police filed into the bedroom. They looked around. Another one walked in with a dog. One of them yelled towards the living room.

"There's no one here!" A policeman in the living room yelled back annoyed.

"Where the fuck did they go? The door was locked from the inside. Unless they sprouted wings, they have to be here somewhere." Alex and Jared stood completely still against the wall. They watched the police flip the bed over. They opened the bedroom closet door and tossed the clothes in the closet onto the floor. Jared made a grimace when his clothes hit the floor. Alex could hear him mumble, "asshole."

One of the policemen startled Alex when he leaned against the wall Jared had formed.

"They're not here. Even the dog isn't picking up anything," the police officer said as he picked up a picture on Jared's dresser. It was a picture of Jared holding another guy very affectionately. The officer looked disgusted, and tossed the picture back on the dresser. Alex looked at Jared and saw his fist clench in anger. After the officer's had left, the square wall started to fade. Alex breathed a sigh of relief and moved away from the wall.

"We need to find out more about this Idol. I think I know where we can get more information about it." Jared started to pull out his phone.

"You wanna google 'death Idol'?" Jared joked laughing.

"No!" Alex snapped. He was annoyed. He didn't see any humor in this situation they were in.

"I have a friend who studies ancient artifacts. He can at least help us find someone who may know something about the Awari." Alex realized that Jared was looking down at his cell phone.

"Jared?" Alex called his name to get his attention. There was impatience in his tone.

"Hey! Are you listening to me?" Jared's attention was deeply concentrated on his phone screen.

"Jared! What are you doing?" Alex moved in closer and realized Jared was actually doing a Google search. He rolled his eyes at Jared. His gray eyes looked at Alex.

"Hey, what do we have to lose? It's a start, right?" He smirked and smiled. A mound of tension left Alex as he laughed a little. It was the first time he'd laughed in what felt like forever.

"Do you have any food in this place? All this drama is making me hungry." Alex couldn't remember the last meal he'd had. It had been a long, strange day.

Alex watched Jared form a wall over the doorway the policemen had just kicked in. He then formed a wall over the wall he'd mistakenly blown out earlier. Alex was exhausted. He sat on a bar stool and watched Jared start making sandwiches.

"Why do you think this is happening?" Alex asked then attacked his sandwich.

"Why does anything happen?" Jared shrugged in confusion opening the refrigerator door.

"Don't you find it strange that it's happening to us? I mean, there are millions of people in New York." Alex took another huge bite of his sandwich.

"I'm sure other people touched the Awari when it was on the vendors' table in Mexico, yet I could only sense you." Jared turned towards Alex with a serious look on his face.

"I think I'm your dead wife reincarnated." Jared's expression went from serious to almost laughing. Alex blinked in surprise. He couldn't believe Jared was making a joke about this. What he'd just said was actually making sense, even though he was acting so casual about it.

"Jared, come on, be serious. I can sense those creatures now. I can sense you. Other people picked up the Awari at the yard sale, but I don't feel them. There must be a reason." Alex said sternly, trying to get Jared to take things seriously.

Jared didn't respond. He reached over and grabbed a bottle of wine. He opened it and put it up to his lips to drink.

"Don't you use a glass?" Alex asked shaking his head. He was realizing Jared was a little too relaxed about things.

"Why?" Jared asked handing Alex the wine bottle.

"I think after the day we had, we should be drinking right out of the bottle." Jared wiped wine from his mouth with his sleeve. Alex had to admit that day had been crazy. He took the bottle from Jared's hand.

"I think you're right," Alex looked at the rim of the bottle, then took a huge gulp of wine.

Jared sat down on the barstool next to Alex.

"In all seriousness, I do feel very drawn to you. I keep feeling like I want to protect you for some reason." Jared turned towards Alex.

"Chris told me about you running out of the club." Alex said, trying to change the subject. Jared was sitting close to him. Alex felt like it was too close, too familiar.

"Yeah. That was the first night I saw those things." Alex took another swig of wine as Jared continued.

"I was dizzy and thought Chris had slipped something into my drink. But after one of those things smacked me across the bathroom floor, I knew that shit was real. I ran out of the bathroom and saw another one standing on the dance floor. It had red eyes."

"What did you do?" Alex asked finishing up his sandwich.

"I tried to find Chris when I saw myself in the mirror and realized my eyes were glowing. Then the symbols came, and the blocks started forming. It was weird. It felt natural for them to form. I swear, sometimes it feels as if the blocks almost react on their own."

"Really?" Alex was intrigued.

"I mean they react in an instant sometimes. I can control them, of course, but it just feels like, I don't know. Like they also somehow think on their own a little. I can't explain it. I guess those things didn't expect it because they looked confused when the blocks started forming. I was able to shoot the blocks in their direction, knocking both creatures back. I felt so cool doing it."

Alex got up and walked over to the sofa. He thought about the events of the last twenty-four hours. He still couldn't believe it. Jared sat down next to him.

"I was really sorry to hear about Daniel. How did you guys meet? It was clear when I met you guys that you had so much chemistry." Alex was shocked that

Jared had turned the conversation to Daniel. Alex had tried to keep the subject of Daniel locked away until all this Awari business was handled. He didn't think he could talk about him yet without crying. He looked at Jared and realized he was trying to take Alex's mind off everything. Alex was grateful and thought maybe talking about Daniel would be therapeutic. He sighed and got comfortable.

"Well, we knew each other since we were teenagers. We started out as best friends in high school. We did everything together. Daniel's father never understood or wanted to understand him. His father was a drunk and his mom passed when he was kind of young. He was the sweetest guy I had ever known. He always put other people's needs over his own."

Alex smiled at a memory that popped into his head about Daniel.

"I remember him telling me he drove forty minutes away from his job to New York, just to help this homeless person he'd just met. He ended up taking the homeless man to dinner at an expensive restaurant. He also gave him some pocket money. Daniel said it was one of the best nights of his life. Daniel used to say that people just wanted to know they are seen. That they are heard and treated like they matter. I admired him so much. He was sincere in everything he did."

Alex got lost in his memories. Jared got up and grabbed another bottle of wine. This time he pulled out two wine glasses.

"I think I gravitated towards Daniel so much because of his home life. My family was so close, that hearing about his childhood was shocking to me. His dad wasn't a good caregiver and very cold towards him. He used to say that he was a ghost to his dad. His mom died when he was young, but he told me he remembered a little bit about her. She was loving, but distant in many ways. Daniel used to say she seemed to be in a constant state of shock."

Jared gave Alex a glass of wine. Alex closed his eyes and savored the deep flavor of the red wine. Talking about Daniel was soothing. Even though talking about him in the past tense hurt so much, just reminiscing about him felt good.

"He told me that his parents never recovered from something that happened to them in the past. Daniel was never sure what that was. All he knew was it took a huge toll on his mom. My mom loved him. My hippie mom and truck driver dad gave Daniel as much love as they gave me. It's so funny that my dad was away all the time, yet I felt more love and closeness with him than Daniel did with a dad that lived with him. He was at our house for dinner almost every night. He became part of the family pretty quick."

Jared leaned back into the sofa, getting more comfortable while he listened. He hadn't interrupted Alex once. He sensed that Alex needed this. The last few weeks had been crazy for both of them. It was nice to have some type of normalcy. They were going to have to figure out what to do about all of this craziness happening to them. But for now, they could just enjoy a normal conversation.

"Am I talking to much? I feel like I'm talking a lot." Alex smiled embarrassed and took a big gulp of wine.

"Not at all. It's nice. I didn't know Daniel well. Hearing about him makes me feel like I'm getting to know him somehow. He sounds like he was a great guy." Alex smiled and shook his head in agreement.

"The year I went to college was rough. I missed seeing Daniel every day. At one point, I couldn't take the distance and invited him up for a visit. I will always remember how surprised he seemed on the phone. He thought I would forget about him once I went to college. When his car pulled up, I remember how happy I was to see him. I went to school in a small college town. I showed him around the town and the campus. We hung out all day. One of my friends there let us drag inner tubes out of his shed. We drifted down the river without a care in the world. He told me he missed me. I remember looking up at the sky and telling him I missed him too. I always regretted not looking at him when I told him that."

Jared refilled Alex's glass. He nodded his thank you.

"When he laughed, his eyes would laugh too. I know how corny that sounds, but it's true. Sometimes I felt sad when he laughed because I knew how sad he truly was inside. He had a way of keeping people at a distance but also making them feel extremely cared for. He had a gift, I swear." Alex let the tears fall.

"The night he was leaving to go back home it started to rain. I walked him down to his car. I remember the moon being so bright that night. There was a soccer field you had to walk across to get to the parking lot. It started to rain. We started running down the steps towards the field when I missed a step and fell. I thought Daniel would laugh, but he ran over to me looking so scared and worried. He helped me up and stood in front of me in the rain. He just looked me in the eyes. I thought he was going to say something, but he didn't. He reached for my hand and folded his fingers in mine. We walked across the field in the rain hand in hand. We reached his car, and he gave me a long hug. He was crying. I only know because I could feel his body trembling. He whispered in my ear that he missed me so much. He pulled back from me as if he didn't want me to see him crying. He turned his back to me and said, "see ya later." He got in the car and drove off. I started back to my dorm. I felt confused, scared, and nervous. When I reached my dorm, I grabbed my cell phone and called Daniel. I paced around the dorm room as the phone rang. He answered and I remember feeling so nervous. I asked him where he was. He told me that he was a few miles away. I told him to pull over at the next rest stop. He sounded confused. I asked him to please pull over and wait for me to get there. I grabbed the keys to my car and ran down the steps. The rain was coming down so hard that the streets were flooding. I gripped the steering wheel so hard that it left indentations in my hands. I saw the sign for the rest stop where he was parked."

"This is like listening to a movie, ha-ha," Jared said intrigued. Alex laughed and held out his glass for another refill. He continued.

"I jumped out of my car and tapped on his window. He reached over to unlock the door. I jumped in and shivered. The rain was so cold. He had the heat on full blast, and it felt so good. Daniel looked at me and started crying. He looked down at his hands and told me that he loved me. Now, at this time, we weren't dating. We were just friends, but we both felt like there was something more between us. Neither of us had ever said anything about it or acted on it. So, when he told me he loved me, I was in shock. He kept crying. He said he missed me so much and felt so lost without me. At that moment I knew what I had to do. I leaned over the seat and kissed him. It was the most amazing kiss. It was slow and passionate. Every emotion between us came out in that first kiss. I forgot about time. I looked him in the eyes and told him that I loved him too. After that we were inseparable. Daniel didn't want to be away from me any longer, so he moved to town the following month. He got a job on campus. I loved leaving my dorm and going to his small apartment in town. It was our own little love nest.

I went home to see my family less and less. Over time, my mom figured out that I had met someone. I was very nervous to tell her who it was, but I was also very proud. She wasn't surprised at all, ha-ha. All she said was, "At least I know who's coming to dinner." she said laughing. I was grateful that she was accepting. My dad also began to think of Daniel as a second son. They even took fishing trips. It felt great knowing my family cared for him.

"Daniel and I had an amazing five years together, but Daniel couldn't open up completely. He never could escape his emotionless upbringing. He was my soul mate. I loved him deeply. I can't picture myself loving another person the way I loved him. Everything should have turned out differently. I don't know if I'll ever get over his death, but I know that I have to learn to live with it. That's what he would have wanted. For me to move on and continue to live my life. I'm trying, but it's so hard. Especially now." Alex gestured to the both of them, referring to everything surrounding the Awari.

"I need to find out what exactly happened to Daniel. He deserved better than this."

Jared stood up and collected their empty wine glasses.

"Look Alex, I know things have been hard for you. We will get through this and we will do it for Daniel." Jared gave Alex a reassuring smile.

"Thank you." Alex felt overwhelmed with emotion. He stood up and gave Jared a hug. Jared accepted it and gave his shoulder a light squeeze when they broke apart.

"You look tired, why don't you go lay down." Jared suggested.

"Do you think that's a good idea right now?"

"We aren't going to be able to fight or do anything if we're tired. We may have new powers, but they don't include superhuman endurance." Alex reluctantly agreed with Jared. It had been a long, tiring day. Alex was so tired, he couldn't even remember the last time he'd slept.

Jared led Alex down the hallway to his bedroom. Alex had a thought, and suddenly stopped.

"You should rest first, and I'll keep watch. I seem to be able to sense those things." Jared shook his head no and pushed Alex towards the bedroom.

"I can defend us better, so I'll keep the first watch," Jared said sternly. Alex climbed into the bed, but didn't think this was a good idea.

Jared's bed felt amazing to Alex. He relaxed for the first time in a long time. He could feel himself drifting off to sleep. Not long after, he was dreaming. He could feel Daniel's hand in his. They were walking to Daniel's car, just like the day he confessed his love for him. The sun cast a warm light down that was so comforting. Daniel was talking about planning a trip to Mexico. He was so excited. He ran a little ahead of Alex and turned to face him. He kept saying how amazing it would be to explore the ruins and caves of Mexico. Alex walked closer to him. Daniel started to cough. He bent over and started coughing uncontrollably. Alex put his hand on Daniel's back and asked him was he okay. Alex could not see his face. He ran his fingers through Daniel's hair. Alex kept telling him that everything would be alright. Alex felt Daniel's body jerk and then black sludge splashed on the ground. It had come from Daniel's mouth. He kept coughing and more hit the ground. Alex called Daniel's name over and over. A deep grumble came from Daniel's body. Daniel answered him, but it was not Daniel's voice. He turned his head to look up at Alex. He had glowing red eyes. Alex jumped back. Daniel just stood there smiling with those red eyes.

Alex opened his eyes to see Jared sleeping next to him in the bed. He was disoriented for a second, then remembered he was in Jared's bedroom. Alex immediately felt something was off. He looked up and saw three of those creatures standing at the foot of the bed. They had sickles and were holding them in the air.

"JARED!" Alex screamed as Jared opened his eyes. Lightning fast, a square formed a wall around the bed, around them. The creatures brought the sickles down to attack them. They broke off once they hit the wall. The creatures yelled and started pounding on the wall furiously.

"Thank god you formed this thing around us. I told you to let me take the first watch. Your ass fell asleep!" Alex was angry and scared and was taking it out on Jared. The creatures pounded harder and harder.

"How strong are your walls, Jared?" Jared looked nervous for the first time since they'd met.

"I don't know," the veins in his neck started to bulge from exertion.

"I feel like I'm in a damn coffin! We can't stay here all night. More came into the room. Alex counted seven.

"What should we do?" Jared looked over his shoulder at Alex in a panic. An idea popped into Alex's head. It was crazy. It was risky. He didn't know if it would work, but he was willing to risk it. He would rather they went out their own way than at the hands of these creatures.

"Jared, can you form a wall around each of us individually?" Jared closed his eyes and a wall started to form between them. Alex could see the bright blue coming from Jared's eyes.

Alex closed his eyes and tried his best to block everything happening out. He could feel energy building inside of himself. He thought of Daniel and a calm came over him. He could see his body starting to glow. A rush of heat flooded his skin. He looked at Jared.

"What are you doing?" Jared's glowing eyes looked at Alex's glowing body in amazement. The creatures pounded harder and harder.

"When I tell you to, drop my wall," Alex yelled through clenched teeth.

"Are you serious?" Jared screamed out.

"Yes! Drop the wall when I say," Alex could feel the energy growing inside. The creatures appeared as energy signatures. Alex could see them through the glow as blobs of red heat. He put his hands over his chest.

94

"Now!" Alex yelled to Jared.

"Are you sure?" he sounded uncertain.

"DO IT NOW!" Jared dropped the wall exposing Alex to the creatures. Alex opened his eyes and released the energy he had built up. The creatures looked startled. One of them tried to reach for Alex, but the energy he'd released exploded, forcing them back. One of them yelled out in pain. He did his best to project the energy outward towards the creatures and away from Jared. He could only hope his walls were holding up to protect him. He looked to the corner of the room and one of the creatures was only partially burned. He rushed towards Alex who let out a blast directly in his direction. The creature started to talk while he was being incinerated.

"We can bring back Daniel!"

"What?" Alex asked in shock. The creature smiled as he burned.

"There is a price." Alex watched his body burn and drift apart.

Chapter 9

Ashes flew around the room. Jared dropped his wall and sat up.

"That was fucking awesome!" he yelled in excitement.

"Where the fuck did they come from?" Jared asked loosening his stiff shoulders.

"I thought you were going to keep watch." Alex said with an attitude. They could have been killed while they slept. Alex was still amped up from the energy he'd just used. Jared just looked at him.

"Man, I only wanted to get a few minutes rest. How was I supposed to know the fucking army of the dead would show up?" Jared said defensively. Alex took a deep breath. He didn't want to fight with Jared. They had enough to worry about without them bickering.

"I know. I'm sorry. But we have to be more careful from this point on." Jared agreed.

"We need to go," Alex said jumping out of the bed.

"Go where?" Jared asked.

"To New York to see my friend Ron. We need answers about these things and that damn Awari."

They gathered and packed as little as possible so they could travel light. Jared grabbed bottled waters and crackers. Alex tried his best to focus. He tried to sense if any more of those creatures were on their way. They peaked out the doorway and looked down the hall. They slowly started making their way down the hallway.

"Oh shit, I almost forgot." Jared turned and ran back to his condo. Alex panicked and ran back with him.

"Is everything okay?"

"I almost forgot my stash," Jared smiled as he put magnum condoms and a bag of weed in his bag.

"Are you serious, Jared?" Alex asked incredulously.

"At a time like this, that's what you're worried about? We could literally be killed any second." Alex couldn't believe him.

"I ain't dead yet." Jared winked at Alex and walked towards the condo doorway. Alex turned to follow Jared and stopped. He started to feel pressure in his head.

"Something is wrong. I feel an energy signature that's similar to ours, but it's different somehow." Jared looked at Alex in confusion.

"Well, where is it?"

"It's headed our way. It definitely isn't one of those creatures. It's something else. I'm having trouble pinpointing it." Alex rubbed his temples and tried to focus.

"Seriously, it's hard to focus on keeping track of this thing." Jared started to speak. Alex put his hand up to stop him.

"Be quiet for a second. I think I have it. It's close." Alex took a deep breath and concentrated harder.

Jared's eyes started to glow. Alex could see blocks forming behind Jared. Alex kept getting flashes of the temple. They were quick, but he was sure it was the temple he was seeing.

Could it be Isic returning? Alex thought to himself.

"You might want to form a wall around the door frame just to be on the safe side." Alex whispered. Jared nodded his understanding. Some of the blocks behind him flew past Alex and split off into multiple blocks. They formed against the doorframe almost as if they were forming a puzzle.

"Where is it?" Jared whispered.

"It must be in the elevator." Alex took a few steps back.

"What does this thing look like?" Jared asked, moving closer to Alex.

"I can't see it like that. I see the structure of the building, like a blueprint. I can see an energy signature in the elevator. I can kind of feel it too, but it's hard to keep my focus on it."

"Can you tell if it's coming here to kill us?" Jared asked in apprehension.

"No, I can't feel its intentions, but I can tell you that there is something familiar about it." Jared's eyes grew brighter.

"It feels so familiar," Alex said under his breath. Jared squared his shoulders, ready to fight.

"It's walking down the hallway. It's about thirty feet away from us."

"Man, shouldn't you be powering up? It seems like it takes some work for you to get in fight mode." Jared said in a rushed voice. Alex got annoyed, but Jared was right. He started to release the rush of energy within himself. Alex started to glow. There was a knock on the newly formed door. Jared and Alex were both powered up now. Alex could feel his teeth grinding. Jared's hands balled up like fists. He had blocks floating around him that took the form of daggers.

"I'm going to fuck this thing up!" Jared was trying to sound brave, but Alex could tell he was nervous. Beads of sweat were dripping down his forehead. There was a knock on the door again. A voice called out.

"Guys? I know you're in there." It was a female's voice.

"What the fuck?" Jared mouthed to Alex. Alex shrugged, just as confused as Jared.

"Guys let me in. I just ran from one of those red eyed things. I'm exhausted and would love to use your bathroom right now."

"What the hell?" Jared and Alex looked at each other. Alex recognized the voice, but couldn't remember who it belonged to.

"Jared drop your wall. If that was a creature, she wouldn't be asking to come in." Jared agreed and dropped the walls and daggers he had created.

They both walked apprehensively to the door. Jared took a breath, then pulled the condo door open. They both stood in stunned silence at the sight before them. Standing at Jared's condo door was a beautiful black woman, with long flowing black hair. She was young, possibly in her early twenties. Her face was so familiar, but Alex couldn't figure out why. She had on a leather jacket and large silver hoop earrings. Alex looked down and saw that she had on stylish suede boots that went up to her knees. She was wearing dark jeans and a t-shirt that perfectly formed to her body. Her large breasts didn't fit her small frame. She was wearing a necklace that matched her earrings. Alex couldn't help but notice her almond shaped eyes. Alex didn't have to be straight to see how sexy she was. She exuded self-confidence. She stomped her feet, bringing Jared and Alex's attention back to her eyes. They had both been transfixed by her beauty.

"Are you going to just stand there staring at me, or are you going to show me to the bathroom? I don't want to be taking a dump if those things show up again. I'm not trying to be killed on the toilet." Her voice was laced with attitude. Any sophistication Alex saw in her, quickly went out of the window the minute she started talking.

"Sure. Here you go princess," Jared's sarcasm was thick. He rolled his eyes while walking her down the hallway to the bathroom. Jared came back and him and Alex shared a surprised look.

"I can't believe I'm letting someone I don't know shit in my bathroom."

"I'm sure far worse things have happened in that bathroom." Alex gave Jared a knowing look and they both laughed. They heard the toilet flush, and turned to see the woman walking towards them.

101

"Well, it's nice to see my parents getting along," she said smiling.

"What the hell are you talking about, Barbie doll?" Jared asked with an attitude. It was clear these two did not like each other already.

"Who are you calling a doll? You're a goth wannabe motherfucker! Your clothes say goth, but your apartment says Martha Stewart!" Jared's eyes widened in shock at her insult. She was quick and witty with her comeback. Alex realized at that moment who she was.

"This is Jared." Jared rolled his eyes a little and nodded. Alex opened his arms to her.

"I was wondering when you would recognize me," she hugged Alex tight. He smiled in her embrace.

"Hi Alicia."

Chapter 10

"Five minutes!" Alicia yelled up the stairs at her little brother, Aaron. The school had already called twice about his tardiness, she wasn't letting him be late again. Sometimes she felt more like his mom than his older sister. She loved it, though. Aaron was a little brat sometimes, but Alicia loved him more than life itself. Their parents had died in a fire when Aaron was just a baby. Alicia remembered vividly her mother screaming for her to get Aaron and run. Alicia's fear and adrenaline kicked in, and she ran like a track star to get her baby brother out of his crib. She made it out of the apartment building, just to see the ceiling collapse in on the building. Alicia watched in numb silence as her parents, and all the other tenants trapped inside, succumbed to the fire. She looked down at the newborn baby in her hands and held him tighter. She vowed she would always be there for him and always protect him. Of course, that wasn't always easy. Once they moved in with their grandmother, Aaron became a little terror. Well not exactly, but he was definitely a hand full. That was partly Alicia's fault. She felt like she had to spoil him and let him get away with a lot to fill her parents' shoes. When Aaron was school age, he started asking about their parents. Alicia knew lying to him would be too hard, but telling him the truth was even harder. So she told him their parents had passed away saving them from a fire. That was the truth, but left out some of the more horrific details.

"I thought you had work," Aaron said running down the steps and jumping into Alicia's arms. She hadn't told him she was coming over. Their grandmother had told her about the school calling, so she made a surprise trip over. She was swamped with studying for the bar, but she would always make time for her grandmother and Aaron. Alicia held Aaron tight and smiled into his shoulder. He was everything to her.

"I do, but I wanted to make sure you made it to school on time. The school called gran twice already." Alicia arched her brow and gave Aaron a stern look. He looked away and down at his shoes.

"I know, she told me." He spoke in a low tone and wouldn't give her eye contact. Alicia knew her brother better than anyone, and knew something wasn't right.

"Hey, what's going on? Talk to me." She put her hand under his chin, forcing him to look at her. Aaron took a deep breath and turned his light brown eyes on Alicia.

"First period is calculus. I hate it! I don't understand it, and the teacher rolls her eyes when I ask her to repeat something. It's embarrassing not knowing." Alicia felt sadness and anger. Sadness that Aaron was struggling in school so much he was willing to be late to miss class. And angry at the teacher for being impatient with a student that needed help. Alicia put on a smile she didn't feel and pulled Aaron close to hug him again.

"I'll tutor you. You're going to be better at calculus than the teacher by the time we're done." Alicia smiled as Aaron laughed at her ridiculous joke.

"But you have school and work. How are you going to have time to help me?"

"I always make time for you. You know you're my favorite person," Aaron smiled and hugged her tight.

"I love you Ally," he'd been calling her that since he first learned to talk. He couldn't pronounce her full name, so she's shortened it for him.

"I love you too. Now let's go. And next time, talk to me if you're having issues at school. It shouldn't take gran to call me for me to find all this out." Alicia passed him his backpack and walked towards the door.

"You're right. I'll come straight to you, I promise. Thanks for taking me to school. I missed you," Aaron grabbed her hand and followed her to her car. Alicia loved her brother so much. She dropped Aaron off at school and beeped the horn when he turned around to wave goodbye. She made her way back to campus. Law school was so demanding that she didn't know how she was going to tutor Aaron. She was going to figure it out though.

She parked in the student parking lot, and jogged to class. She was late.

From a very young age, Alicia knew she wanted to either be a lawyer or a politician. She loved to talk and debate. Her parents were amazed at how she would negotiate for more allowance money, or debate about why certain chores didn't matter. They always encouraged her and that really helped stoke her inner confidence. After finding out the building her parents died in had faulty wiring, Alicia knew she was going to be a lawyer. There was no way she was going to let people get away with neglecting safety issues.

The only problem was that she couldn't afford school. She wouldn't dare ask her grandmother to take out a loan or put up her house for collateral. So she worked as many jobs as she could. Her favorite was the campus bookstore. She met so many different people and had a lot of freedom. It was great. One of her favorite co-workers was Daniel. He was so kind and gentle, he reminded her of Aaron. Alicia felt protective of him. One time a rowdy customer said a homophobic slur to Daniel. Alicia cursed him out so bad, he ran out of the store halfway in tears. Sweet Daniel had stayed calm and collected the whole time the guy was disrespecting him. He really was one of a kind. A higher paying job opened up in the student housing office, so Alicia quit the bookstore. On her last day, Daniel gave her a card and a CD. She laughed because she didn't even think people still listened to CDs. She saw him around campus a few more times, but after her workload got heavier, they lost touch.

She didn't know he'd died until she saw a memorial for Daniel at the campus bookstore. She cried all night. She heard that his boyfriend Alex was going to be having a yard sale of his things. She thought it would be good for her to go. She wanted to have something of Daniel's as a keepsake. He had been such a sweet friend to her, she couldn't fathom him suddenly dying so young. It made her think of her parent's untimely death.

She wandered around the yard sale trying to decide what to get. She saw a blue t-shirt he wore a lot on a rack. She ran her fingers over the fabric and smiled. She continued walking around, until she saw a weird looking statue. It was creepy and ugly. She couldn't imagine this being something of Daniel's. She picked it up and turned it over in her hands, trying to see what was written on it. It was warm. She started feeling a little nauseous. She put the little statue down and walked back to her car. She decided she couldn't handle having something of Daniel's. It would just remind her of his death. That made her sad all over again.

A few days passed and Alicia noticed she was feeling nauseous more and more. She thought maybe her course load and multiple jobs were stressing her out. Something that always made her feel better was pampering herself. She booked a hair and nail appointment for the next day.

"Hey Alicia! Haven't seen you in a long time. Law school must be kicking your ass," her stylist laughed and walked her to her chair. Alicia laughed and shook her head in agreement. Her stylist draped a shampoo cape around her neck. Alicia watched her in the mirror and then her vision became blurry. Alicia blinked a few times and realized her stylist was wearing an apron and had a white bonnet on her head. She had a yellow glow around her. They weren't in the salon anymore. They were in a cold kitchen. It looked to be right out of the eighteen hundreds. Alicia looked at her stylist again and saw that she was kneading bread, like a baker.

Alicia's heart started beating faster and faster.

"What the hell is going on?" The stylist took a loaf of bread out of the oven and started humming. Alicia realized she was looking at her stylist from the past. Like she was seeing who she was in a past life. Alicia blinked again, and the stylist was brushing her hair, talking like nothing had just happened.

What the fuck? Alicia said to herself as she tried to figure out what just happened. She tried to calm down and think logically. She was a law student. Her mind was wired to see facts and logic. What she just saw was the opposite of both. She got through her hair appointment and made her way to the nail salon. She couldn't shake the feeling that something was going on inside of her. When she opened the door to the nail salon, her vision got blurry again. Every nail technician was glowing blue and had turned into Geisha's. Alicia lost her footing as she backed out of the nail salon. It was happening again. She was seeing people as they were in their past lives.

107

Alicia drove back to campus with her mind all over the place. She was walking towards the campus library when she saw an older woman walking towards her. She didn't look familiar.

"Your aura smells lovely," her creepy voice felt like bugs on Alicia's skin.

"I almost couldn't sense you. Tricky girl."

"Excuse me?" Alicia turned towards her and realized her eyes were red and glowing. Alicia's fear heightened. She watched the woman's face start to contort into something resembling a goblin.

"Get away from me!" Alicia screamed and ran back towards her car. She heard footsteps chasing her. Her heart was pumping fast as she raced across the parking lot. She was about four feet away from her car, when she saw something black out of the corner of her eye. She slowed down and looked at the object. It was her hand! It was completely black. And so were her legs. She stopped completely and looked herself over. Her whole body was completely black, like a crow. Panic started to rise inside of her. A sound startled her. She remembered she was being chased. Alicia turned around as the grotesque woman reached her. Something inside her told her to protect herself. A burning sensation built up inside of her. Alicia rushed the woman and grabbed her by the shoulders. The woman's eyes widened in shock. Alicia picked her up like she weighed nothing. Little white bumps popped up on her arms and grew out like spikes. They started to intertwine around the creature and pierce her skin. The spikes went through every inch of her body, and made a hard crunching sound when it went through the creature's head. Stunned herself, Alicia tossed the dead woman across the parking lot just as easily as she would toss a rock. *Wow,* she said to herself. She watched the woman go airborne for a few seconds, then snapped out of her shock. She felt the fire inside of her start to come down and her skin color returned. She looked around the parking lot and was thankful it was still empty.

108

She did a light jog to her car. She peeled out of the parking lot and drove towards her apartment. She broke out into a cold sweat. *What's happening to me?* She asked herself as she drove faster and faster. Since the other day, nothing had been the same. She wondered what had happened to make her think she was going crazy. She retraced her steps in her head. The only thing she'd done out of the ordinary was go to that yard sale. But all she'd done was touch Daniel's shirt and pick up that ugly statue. That ugly statue had burned in her hands and made her feel sick almost immediately. Alicia had a bad feeling about that statue.

All of a sudden she remembered hearing that one of Chris's friends named Jared had some type of freak out at a club. She'd seen him at the yard sale that day. Could it be a coincidence? Alicia didn't believe in coincidences, so she knew she needed to talk to Jared. She ran into her apartment and straight to the bathroom to splash water on her face. She looked at herself in the mirror. She couldn't see any physical changes, but something was different about her. Her eyes started to get glassy. Suddenly, she wasn't in her bathroom. She was inside of a temple. A weird ritual was playing out in front of her eyes. She saw people and things she didn't know or understand. Alicia felt like she was seeing things from the eyes of a child. The names Itzel and Acan kept running through her brain. She was standing on top of a cliff and saw her hands throwing something off. It was the ugly statue. *Awari.* The word came out of her mouth. Alicia's vision came back. She felt breathless. She needed to get to Jared quick. But first she needed to make sure these newfound abilities were under control. She didn't want to be around anyone and suddenly turn black. Especially not Aaron or their grandmother.

She laid low while she tried to conjure up the powers, and then make them go away. After a little while, Alicia felt like she had some sort of control over them. Other things happened over that time. Those little white spikes would spring out of her

109

arm at random times. Or she would realize that she wouldn't get tired after running on the treadmill for a long time. She could also bounce off things. Like her body was rubber. It seemed like new powers kept manifesting every few hours. It was time to get to the bottom of this. After some time, she felt like she was ready to leave her apartment. On her way to her car, she spotted a man with glowing red eyes walking towards her. She quickly jumped into her car and put it into gear. After getting Jared's address from Chris, she pulled up outside his condominium to pure chaos.

There were police, ambulances, and a coroner's van. Rubble and debris were all over the sidewalk. There was no way she was going through the front door. She looked at the lobby window in surprise. It was completely shattered. A tenant came out of the building and Alicia quickly slipped into the building when they came out. She took the stairs and knocked on Jared's door. It looked like glass. She could see an outline of two figures and hear voices behind the door.

Chapter 11

"You know each other?" Jared asked surprised. Alex let go of Alicia and nodded.

"She worked with Daniel at the college bookstore. I haven't seen you in so long, I couldn't put a name to the face." Alex smiled at Alicia again. For some reason, seeing one of Daniel's friends put a smile on his face.

"It's been years, I know. Oh, um, I was really sorry to hear about Daniel." Alex nodded and closed his eyes. They started to burn with fresh tears. He cleared his throat and willed the tears away.

"I wanted to catch up with you before now, but some interesting things have happened. So unfortunately, this isn't a social call." Alicia walked over to the refrigerator and pulled out a bottled water.

"Daniel was such a sweet guy. We all loved him at work. He had a way of making everyone feel important." It hurt Alex to hear Alicia talking about Daniel in the past tense. She flipped her hair over her shoulders and started smiling at a memory.

"I loved that he never tried to be anything other than himself. He was real." She took another sip of the water.

"On his last day he gave me a CD of songs he thought I might like. It sat on my dresser at home for months because I don't really use my CD player. One rainy night I decided to listen to it." She looked them in the eyes.

"The songs were so deep and like nothing I had ever heard before. The words were amazing. I felt like I was getting to know Daniel through those songs. I wanted to call him after that, but I didn't have his number. I should have tried harder to reach out. The next thing I know, it's years later and I hear about his death." Her voice quivered.

"I found out about the yard sale. I felt like I should have something of his, but I chickened out."

Alex looked at her and pulled the idol out of a bag.

"Do you remember touching this?"

"Oh my god! Yes! I remember thinking it was ugly. That's what's causing all of this." She got up from the bar stool and walked over to the sofa and sat down.

"Days after the yard sale a bunch of weird things started happening to me. Little white things started sticking out of my arms. I also noticed that I could run a long time and not get tired."

"Like how long?" Jared asked intrigued.

"I could run on the treadmill for hours without getting tired or even breaking a sweat."

"Oh, shit!" Jared covered his mouth in surprise. Alicia smiled in amusement at his reaction.

"I know right? I also seemed to be able to bounce off things. If I ran at a door, I could jump feet first and hover in the air for a second. Then I could jump from the door and land perfectly. Like a cat. I had no clue what was happening to me. I thought about going to a doctor, but I didn't want any tests run on me. I don't like needles." Alex and Jared's eyes were glued to her, listening in shock.

"The craziest thing is when I look at people. I see more than just them. I can see their aura. I can see who they were in a past life. It's not like a vision. I clearly see them at that moment, but I also see them as they were in the past. Kind of like looking at two of each person."

"Did your powers let you see that we were here?" Alex asked sitting next to her.

"Nah," she sipped more water.

"I called Chris and he told me that you called about Jared's address and then he gave it to me. I already knew what happened to Jared, so I knew it wasn't a coincidence you went looking for him after that yard sale." Jared looked at Alex in annoyance.

"Did Chris give my address to every person in the city of New York?"

"Apparently." Alicia laughed and took another sip of water.

"What do you mean you knew what happened to Jared?" Alex looked at her in question. She stood up and stretched.

"I heard the story about the freak out at the club. And after one of those things attacked me on my way home from getting my hair done, I figured maybe Jared wasn't crazy. Maybe." She smiled playfully at Jared. He smirked at her.

"How did you get away?" Alex asked walking into the kitchen.

"When it tried to attack me at school, I picked it up like it weighed nothing. White spikes grew out my arms and intertwined around it. The spikes went through her head or whatever that thing was." Alex had grabbed a soda out of Jared's refrigerator.

"So, let me get this straight. You're fast and strong. You can sort of reverse gravity for a second, and you can stab people with spikes that come out of your arms? Oh, and you can see people's pasts?" Alicia nodded her head in amazement.

"Damn. That's a lot." Alex sat down and sighed.

"It sure is," she sighed too.

"And I think I'm invisible to those things. The creature said she had a hard time sensing me. Whatever that meant."

"Yeah, something about you is hard to see. I had a hard time tracking you for some reason." Alex seemed confused at that revelation.

"And my body shifts when I do all these things." Alicia said, watching them carefully. She seemed hesitant to tell them that part.

"What do you mean, 'shift'?" Jared chimed in. Alicia took a deep breath and changed into a black creature with glowing light blue eyes. She had small spikes on

114

her arms and her hair blended into her skin. She looked like an alien. Alex and Jared stared with their mouths open. It was silent in the condo for about three full minutes.

"That's something you don't see every day," Jared said breaking the ice. It unnerved Alex to look at Alicia in her shifted form. Alicia looked at Alex with her glowing eyes. She picked up the Awari. Her glowing eyes looked glassy.

"I can see that you are Acan, and you are Itzel, Jared." Alicia looked at Jared.

"You hid me before they came to take everyone from the village. I was seven years old." Alex listened to Alicia talk. Her voice had changed a little.

"I ran into the temple after the explosion of light. I climbed over tons of rubble to get to where you were Acan. I wanted to save my mom and dad. To save you both. I was tiny, so I could get through places others could not. I found you, Acan, laying on the floor. You asked me to take the idol and throw it into the sea. I took it from your dying hand and ran through the collapsed temple. I stood on a high cliff with the Awari. I remember the wind was so strong. I was small, but I knew I had to throw it with all my might into the ocean. I threw the idol and the wind seemed to carry it. I watched it splash into the ocean. It was supposed to be forever lost at sea. Then..." Alicia looked at Alex in her new form and it made him uncomfortable.

"I can see that the idol laid at the bottom of the sea for a very long time, until it landed on a fisherman's boat after a storm. The idol changed him and him and his ship mate died that night. His wife collected the Awari after coming to claim the body. She decided to sell it at one of the resorts she worked at. I can see Alex picking up the Idol."

"Mrs. Alvarez!" Alex gasped at the story. Alicia could see the Awari's past too it seemed.

"I can also see that the idol is not magic."

"What?" Jared and Alex asked at the same time. Alex looked directly into Alicia's glowing eyes.

"If it's not magical, then what the hell is it?"

"It's alien," she said handing the idol back to Alex.

"I'm assuming you guys know there is another part of the idol missing right?" Alex and Jared nodded yes.

"In my other life, I saw that the other half of the idol was still buried deep inside the temple. The temple is in Mexico. We have to bring the idols together to end all of this." Alicia shifted back into her natural form. Alex was relieved at that.

"Are you telling me we have to go to Mexico? And then dig in some ancient temple? And after that, connect these things and see what happens?" Jared asked incredulously. Alex rubbed his temples. He felt a headache coming on. It seemed like every time they came closer to figuring out how to end this, another obstacle was put in their way.

"First we should go to see my friend Ron. He's at NYU right now. He can help us get more answers about this thing." Alex tried to calm Jared down. Jared grabbed the idol from his hand.

"You'd better be right," he put the idol in his bag.

"A lot of people's lives are depending on us figuring this out," Alicia chimed in.

"Yeah, including our own!" Jared put his backpack on and secured it tight. They ran out into the hall to see other tenants gathered around talking. They all turned to look at them. A man with a blue business suit on stopped them as they walked down the hall towards the stairwell.

"Do you know what happened?" The man looked scared.

"We heard a loud explosion. Some people ran out the building thinking it was something connected to terrorism." The man's panic started to rise. Jared looked the man dead in his eyes and said,

116

"It's worse. It's something you can't even imagine." The man gulped and stepped back.

Jared opened the fire escape door and watched Alicia run lightning fast in front of him. "Hey! Stop showing off," Jared yelled at her as she kept running down the steps. Alicia laughed and ran even faster. When Jared and Alex reached the bottom of the stairs, Alicia reached for the door.

"Let me do a scan before we open the door. I don't want to be surprised." Alex stopped her. Alicia backed up. Alex closed his eyes. He could feel the structure of the building. He felt the panic of the people in the building.

"I don't feel any of those creatures in the building or outside. Well, at least not within twenty feet of the building." Alicia looked relieved. Alex remembered he had burned the door handle when he was fleeing the guard earlier. He looked at Alicia, who got the hint.

"Hiya!" Alicia screamed and kicked the door in.

"I always wanted to say that ha-ha!" She laughed as Alex and Jared rolled their eyes at her.

They walked through the lobby, trying to act casual in all of the chaos. Alex saw a policeman checking out the window the manager had been thrown through. *That poor guy had no clue what he stepped into, and ended up dead because of it.* Alex thought about that sadly. He thought about all the people who had been hurt since that damned Awari had been washed up on that boat. Strategically walking around the police and the crowds, they made it outside. They stood on the sidewalk trying to figure out their next move.

"Does anyone have a car out here? Mine is currently surrounded by police, so there's no way we're getting to it." Alicia said looking at Alex and Jared.

"I had a car, but it's busted now after I was attacked earlier. I took a taxi here." Alex said and looked to Jared. He smiled and rubbed his hands together.

"I have a car, but it's in the parking garage three levels down."

"No! I'm not trying to get trapped in a parking garage with those things chasing us." Alicia huffed and folded her arms in defiance.

"We have to get to the car Alicia." Alex put his hand on her shoulder.

"We can't chance having more innocent people get hurt again." She sighed and nodded in agreement. They walked around the corner to the garage.

"Your eyes are glowing," Alicia said to Alex.

"I can feel those creatures coming."

"Shit! How far are they?" Jared asked in a rushed voice.

"Not far enough," Alex grabbed Alicia's hand, pulling her along.

"Let's go!" They ran down the ramp of the garage.

"Those things are within a few feet of us." Alex said frantically, running even faster.

"Should we try and take the elevator? I mean it's right there." Jared said pointing to the elevator door as they continued running.

"Hell no! I don't know about y'all, but I'm taking this ramp." Alicia let go of Alex's hand and ran at full speed down another level.

"We can't risk getting stuck in an elevator." Alex commented as him and Jared ran after Alicia down the ramp.

Just as they reached the third level, they stopped.

"What is that noise?" Alicia asked looking around. Jared looked up as a hood of a car flew over our heads. The hood hit the back wall of the parking garage, and smashed to the ground.

"WHAT THE FUCK! Jared get your car right now!" Alex screamed and ducked for cover. Jared started pushing the button to his alarm and looking around.

"You don't know where you parked?" Alicia asked louder than she should have.

"It's valet parking!" Jared yelled, hitting the button over and over. Alicia put her hand over her eyes. A loud, growling noise echoed throughout the parking garage. They could hear glass breaking and car alarms going off on the level above them.

"Jared! Find your car now!" Alex whispered through clenched teeth. He was getting nervous. Jared hit the button again, and lights on a car in the corner flashed.

"Thank god!" Alicia said relieved. They started running for the car when a huge shadow flew over them. They all stopped when a man who seemed seven feet tall stood in front of them.

"Oh,shit! Who the fuck is this creep?" Alicia asked in annoyance. Alex and Jared exchanged scared glances as they prepared to fight. The man had glowing red eyes. He had on a cowboy hat and a large black trench coat. His skin was grey, and he had something sticking out of his mouth. They watched in horror as something wet dripped from his lips.

"What the hell is in his mouth?" Alicia asked looking out of the corner of her eye.

"Oh my god! It looks like someone's arm." Alex gasped and started backing up. Jared looked just as disgusted as Alex at the sight of the dangling arm. The creature started walking towards them, throwing the arm to the ground. Each step the creature took seemed to shake the floor.

"Alex, where are the other creatures?" Jared whispered, not taking his eyes off the large man in front of them.

"They left. I don't sense them now." Alex felt fear at that realization.

"They must think this thing can do some real damage if they didn't even bother to stay." Jared said starting to form blocks around himself.

Alex started to build up his energy flow. Alicia stood there looking terrified.

"Alicia! change now!" Alex yelled at her.

"What?" She asked in a daze. The creature moved fast and tore a hood off a car. He then threw it at them. Alex ducked and it flew over him. Jared formed his wall and the hood smashed against it. The creature turned and lifted a car and threw it towards Alicia. Alex ran towards Alicia to cover her. Jared formed his wall around them just before the car landed on them.

"Jesus Christ! We have to get out of here!" Alicia's frantic voice shrieked.

"I can't release the wall, or you'll be smashed." Jared started yelling. Alex realized that as long as Jared was protecting them from the car, he couldn't run.

"Guys, I can't always form two large walls at the same time." Jared said reading Alex's mind. He looked from under the wall to see Jared's eyes glowing bright. The creature growled as it ran towards Jared.

Alex looked over to see Alicia changing. Her skin went dark and her eyes started glowing brighter.

"Fuck this!" She ran from under the wall. Alicia tackled Jared just before the creature knocked him to the ground. Much to Alex's surprise, Alicia seemed to be able to hold Jared and float with him sideways. She touched back down to the ground. The creature yelled in frustration and tore a tire off a car to throw it at her. Alex watched in concern as Alicia ducked to the ground. Alicia moved quickly. She jumped from a car to the wall, then to the ceiling within a matter of seconds. She landed behind the creature. In her darkened state, it was difficult to make out her form. It was like she was camouflaged.

The creature made a surprised growling sound as Alicia grabbed it by its left leg. His eyes went wide in shock as Alicia threw the creature into a car. Alex ran from under Jared's wall as Jared released it. The car that was on top of it crashed to the ground.

"Enough of this." Jared started forming four huge blocks. They shifted into the shape of giant spears. The creature seemed dazed and started to stand up from the car Alicia threw it into.

"Do it!" Alicia screamed as Jared released the spears. The creature smiled. The grey skin on the creature started to form black lines, like vines. Millions of lines started forming over its skin. The spears flew through the air towards the creature to pierce him. The black lines on the creature leaked a black tar like substance and formed around its skin. It was like a protective shell. He was now completely black. The spears hit the creature and bounced off his body, landing on the ground.

"No!" Alicia screamed out in anger. She started running towards the creature.

"Jared! Stop her!" Alex yelled frantically as loud as he could. Jared tried to form a wall to block her, but she jumped on and over it. She landed behind the creature again. She moved lightning fast and wrapped her arms around its neck. She was trying to choke it from behind. The creature reached behind it's back and grabbed her. It roughly threw her to the ground. Alex gasped in fear and powered up. Symbols started flowing around the creature. He picked Alicia up and put her in a bear hug facing us.

"Fuck this thing up!" She screamed, struggling in his arms. The creature started laughing.

"What do we do Alex?" Jared's worried voice echoed throughout the garage.

"I can't blast the creature while it's holding Alicia!" They both looked at Alicia yelling at the creature.

121

"You picked the wrong bitch to get up close and personal with!" They watched as Alicia's hair started to grow.

"What the hell is she doing?" Alex asked Jared. Suddenly the creature started yelling out in anguish. His grip started to loosen from Alicia. That was Jared and Alex's cue to run closer to them. Alicia's hair started shifting. It turned into needles. Each strand of hair had hardened. They watched her hair shoot through the eyes of the creature. It stumbled backwards and fell back on the car. Alicia broke free from his grasp and stood in front of the creature. Her hair shifted again into thousands of needles. She shot the needle strands right down the throat of the creature. Alex used his newfound sense to see inside the creature. The needles were piercing the creature's heart over and over. The creature's body twitched, then stopped moving altogether. Alicia retracted her hair and walked towards us like nothing had just happened. Jared walked up to her.

"Another new power?" His voice sounded skeptical. Alex felt like Alicia was holding back more of what she could do.

"Apparently." She walked towards Jared's car. Alex and Jared shared a suspicious look. Jared got in the driver's seat while Alicia jumped in the back seat.

"I love it when I get the whole back seat to myself." She proceeded to put her feet up on the seat to lay down.

"Feet off the seats. This car is worth more than you could imagine," Jared was irritated. Alicia rolled her eyes as Alex buckled his seatbelt. She didn't budge.

"We almost died. This should be the least of your worries." Alicia sucked her teeth and put her hands behind her head.

"Lord, I feel like we are her parents." Jared mumbled starting the car. The car had only gone a few feet when Alex felt a strange sensation.

"Jared, stop the car!"

"Why? We need to get out of here," Jared looked at him like he was crazy.

"That thing's back up just arrived." Alex swallowed the lump in his throat.

"Are you shitting me?" Alicia sat up and looked out the car window. Alex could feel her put her hands on the back of his seat.

"Where? I don't see anything."

"Trust me, they're here. I can feel them." Alex closed his eyes to focus.

"Shit man, you couldn't have sensed them earlier than this?" Jared's fear and frustration was rising. He moved the car forward slowly.

"I'm sorry. I was a little distracted by that giant creature trying to kill us Jared!" Jared's face turned red in embarrassment. *Now was not the time to turn on each other,* Alex thought to himself. He took a breath and tried to soften his tone.

"Sometimes I have to work into sensing these things. It's not always immediate."

"I know. Sorry," Jared apologized, inching the car forward again.

"How fast can you form your walls?" Alex had an idea. A crazy one.

"I don't know, I never timed it. But I'd say pretty quick. Why?" Alex turned to look back at Alicia.

"Don't get out of the car, no matter what happens."

"Okay, that won't be a problem," she said looking directly at me. As brave as she was acting, Alex could sense her fear. That creature had almost crushed her. She had to be feeling all sorts of emotions right now.

"We only have to drive up two more levels to get out of here. I'll yell out the direction of where they are, and you form a wall while driving." Jared looked at Alex like he had four heads.

"That's your plan? Are you serious?" He put his hand on the gear shift. Alex sensed them getting closer.

"Yes I am." Alex tried to sound confident in his plan.

"I'll try. Can't promise anything though," Jared shook his head at the crazy idea again.

"Why don't I just try and form a wall completely around the car?"

"How much energy will you need to keep a wall around us?" Jared sighed, looking drained already.

"More than I can handle right now." Jared admitted.

"I'll help take them out while you're driving Jared," Alicia offered slowly. Alex could tell she didn't want to come into contact with those things again.

"For the record, I've never done this while in a moving car."

"Well, there's a first time for everything right?" Alex tried to joke around, but Jared wasn't amused.

Alicia held onto the back of Alex's seat and closed her eyes as the car started forward. Jared pushed the peddle to the floor and catapulted them forward. Alex could see the creatures on the sides of them trying to run and keep up with the car.

"Jared, wall two o'clock!" Jared formed a wall just in time for a creature to run right into it. They all breathed a sigh of relief at how quick Jared's walls came up. Alex pointed up.

"Twelve o'clock!" They heard a creature land on the wall that Jared formed above them.

Alex looked back to see the floating wall disappear with the creature falling off of it.

Jared turned the wheel as they made it to the second level. Alex concentrated and formed a symbol over one standing in the middle of the ramp. It exploded, taking out another creature standing next to it.

"Cool!" Alicia yelled from the backseat.

"Jared, form a big wall behind us right now!"

Alex could sense a very large creature behind them. He turned to see the top of a very large creature just above Jared's wall. The creature ran yelling into the wall. Alex tried his best to focus on more than one at a time, but it was difficult to pinpoint them and explode them at the same time. Jared swerved around two creatures running towards them. Jared turned the wheel, they were close to getting out of the garage. It was then that Alex sensed something very sinister.

"Stop the car right now!" Alex felt nauseous.

"Why man? We're almost out of here!"

"I said stop the car!" Alex could sense twenty of those things standing on the sides of the ramp. Some of them were sitting on cars waiting.

"Holy shit!" Alicia screamed from the back seat. A voice spoke to them.

"You're not going anywhere."

"Who the hell is that?" Alicia and Jared asked in stunned unison.

"I'm getting out of the car," Alex told them, sounding braver than he felt.

"Are you fucking crazy?" Jared grabbed his arm as he opened the door.

"Trust me." Alex looked him in the eyes and pleaded for him to understand.

"Look man, I don't know you well. But I don't want anything bad to happen to you. *Please* get back in the car." Jared's voice was laced with worry. Alex looked at Alicia's worried face. He had to do this. He felt it deep inside that he was meant to face this thing head on.

"Please trust me. I've got this." Alex said surprisingly calm.

"Jared, form a wall around the car for ten minutes."

"What are you going to do?" Jared let his arm go.

"I'm going to get us out of here. This energy signature seems familiar. I need to get answers." Alex stepped out of the car, then ducked his head back in.

"Keep Alicia safe and hold the wall steady Jared," he watched the wall form around the car after closing the door. Someone was walking towards him. There were a dozen pairs of red eyes looking at him from the sides of the garage. The creatures stayed off to the sides of the ramp, almost like they were waiting for instructions. The person or thing walking towards him was shrouded in shadow.

"Come into the light. Who are you?" He moved into the light of the garage.

"You already know me, Acan." Alex felt a chill rush over him. Goosebumps lined his arms. He knew that voice.

"Oh my god!" *It was him. Isic. That fucking crazy leader from the temple in Mexico! But how?* Questions rushed into Alex's mind as he tried to make sense of this. He looked at his watch, three minutes had passed.

"Oh, Acan. You killed me, only to have me reappear. Stings, doesn't it? But I guess you know a little something about coming back, don't you?" Isic started laughing. Alex closed his eyes. He focused and kept calm.

"What do you want?" Alex asked him without opening his eyes.

"I want to finish what I started, but I can't!" Isic yelled, then tried to compose himself. Alex could hear Isic's voice trembling.

"I can't finish because you have what I need. I want the Awari, and I want it now." His tone was demanding.

"I need to complete the ceremony. I deserve ultimate power." Alex stayed focused, but wanted to get as much information from Isic as he could. He needed to know what Isic meant. Maybe it held the key to destroying him.

"I was cast from one world like trash! Once the power is all mine, I'll seek my revenge." Alex had no idea what he was talking about, but he knew that Isic could never get the Awari. No matter what the cost.

126

Alex could feel the symbols forming. He concentrated and split them off to target multiple creatures. He did his best to block Isic out. Alex now had twelve creatures targeted.

"Why and how did you murder Daniel?" Alex lost focus for a minute to look Isic in the eyes. So much emotion was in his voice. He needed closure about Daniel. Alex would never reconcile with Daniel's death until he got a reason behind it. He was never coming back though, so Alex knew this question was strictly for his heart. Isic smiled and spoke in a very low tone.

"Daniel was just a casualty of war. Just an obstacle in the way of getting the Awari in Mexico." *An obstacle?* Alex fumed inside at how nonchalant Isic was being about the murder of the love of his life. He tried to calm down, but it was almost a losing battle. Isic was still talking, even though Alex was only half listening now.

"The Awari has been lost for a very long time. I created it to improve a situation my son, you, were involved in. However, the Awari started to weaken and needed an energy source to feed its power." Alex looked down at his watch again. Five minutes now gone.

"I learned by accident that trapping souls inside of it enhanced the Awari's powers. I see you look confused. I thought maybe all of Acan's memories had come to you as well as his abilities." Alex glanced down again, six minutes had passed. Isic moved closer and continued.

"The Awari has the ability to enhance a person's mind and abilities if touched. It can contain the memories of the people who have touched it too. One of my favorite things it can do is create physical changes. That's something you've benefitted from I see. It did not destroy us that day in the temple. It absorbed us." Alex blinked in shock. He thought he had witnessed Isic's death in the temple. But he'd only witnessed the Awari consuming him. When Mrs. Alvarez's husband and ship mate touched the Awari, it must have somehow released the trapped souls. Including Isic.

"Acan, Itzel, their daughter and I all touched the Awari at some point. It was made for my family. Made for you," Isic walked closer to Alex.

"I am NOT your family," Alex said through clenched lips. He felt so much pain and anger towards Isic, it was hard to keep concentrating on his plan. Again, Isic laughed at Alex, like a parent laughs at a silly idealistic child.

"Are we not the sum of our memories Acan? Are we not forms of energy? The Awari has the power to transfer and enhance energy. I should know because I created it." It was like a bomb exploded in Alex's head. He stepped back in shock.

"You did?"

"Yes. For you. For my son, Acan. "

"Why? None of this makes any sense!" Alex felt like the walls were closing in on him.

"You know why, Acan."

"STOP CALLING ME THAT!" Alex screamed in frustration.

"You are Acan and not him at the same time. You have his memories and abilities."

"And what abilities did the Awari give you?" Alex tried to see if Isic had an Achilles heel. He seemed impossible to kill. He'd been blown up, only to be reincarnated again.

"Oh, there are so many I've lost count. Every soul it has ever consumed is inside of me. Right now, I'm taking advantage of the ability I have to create and control life."

Isic looked to the right at a group of creatures that had gathered there.

"I create and control my creatures by touch. Like this body I'm in. But it only works on weak or evil minds."

"So, you force evil and darkness into innocent people? Then what? You make them kill people for you?" Alex felt sick to his stomach. Isic smiled so sinister, Alex took another step closer to the car.

"I don't force anything. A trapped soul seeps into whoever touches the Awari or whoever I touch. And that creature absorbs more souls for the Awari. Those souls are not so innocent. The Awari cannot force a soul into just anyone. There has to be something dark or familiar lurking just below the surface for it to grab onto. The more souls it has, the stronger it becomes. You see, me and the Awari share the same power. And one cannot exist without the other. Fortunately, there's a lot of evil souls in this world. Before you took hold of the Awari, so many people had already touched it. And many have touched it afterwards. As the Awari gets stronger, so do I. But I'm tired of sharing the power. I want it all. I need that Awari to complete the power transfer. It's going to take a lot of souls." Isic's eyes lit up thinking about that. Alex thought back to those people tied to the wall in the temple. Isic was stealing all their souls to get all of the Awari's power. He thought back to how Isic had violently killed Itzel and realized that was probably the only way he could get her soul. She wasn't evil, neither him nor the Awari could just absorb it. Alex swallowed the vomit that was trying to come up.

"It didn't change me, Jared or Alicia though," Alex said out loud.

"Do you want to know why that is?" Isic asked in a sing song voice. He dangled the truth in front of Alex, trying to distract him. Alex ignored him and concentrated harder. He could hear the echo of Isic's shoes throughout the garage as Isic got closer to him. Alex had sixteen creatures targeted in his mind. He tried, but could not get a lock on Isic. Some sort of interference was around him. Isic said something Alex didn't respond to. He knew he only had a few minutes before Jared and Alicia would drop the wall from around the car.

"Acan! Listen to your father when I am speaking to you!" Isic's powerful voice boomed, forcing Alex to open his eyes in surprise at the outburst of anger. Alex had locked onto nineteen creatures now. He looked at his watch one final time. Nine minutes had passed. He turned to look at the car. The walls were still around the car. Alex breathed a sigh of relief and started to power up with everything he had. Isic looked at Alex in amusement and then laughed hysterically. Alex tried to ignore him, but a nervousness overcame him. Something felt wrong.

"Oh, Alex. The structure of this building can't handle that blast you're gearing up for." His smug smiled deflated Alex's bravery instantly. He used his power to do a quick scan of the building. Isic was right. There were two support beams directly behind ten creatures. Taking them out, meant caving in the whole garage. Alex's mind raced. *Should I chance it anyway? Nothing was more important than getting rid of Isic and these creatures. Maybe it was worth the risk.* Alex looked back at the car in indecision.

"You can blow up my pets, but the innocent people on the levels below will pay the price. You'll bury them, just as you did to me thousands of years ago."

"FUCK!" Alex knew Isic had him right where he wanted him. Isic knew too. That sinister smiled had not left his face. He walked closer to Alex, giving him a full view of him. Well, a view of the man's body he was inhibiting. He was white, about six foot tall, and obese. He had a black goatee, and wore wire rimmed glasses.

"Acan, give me the Awari or–" walls started forming around Isic. Within seconds, he was entombed in one of Jared's creations.

"Can we go now?" Jared yelled out of the passenger window. Alex jumped in the car. They drove around a fully encased Isic.

130

"What the hell was going on? I thought you had some master plan." Jared asked irritated.

"That was the longest fucking ten minutes of my life!" Alex opened his mouth to tell Jared and Alicia the information he'd just learned when his heart stopped cold. A gagging noise forced his attention to the driver's seat. Jared's face was red as a tomato.

"OH MY GOD!" Alicia screamed as Alex stared in shock. The car swerved as they made it to street level.

"Jared are-are you okay?" Jared coughed, then his eyes rolled into the back of his head.

"SHIT!" Alex screamed at the same time he felt Isic's presence. *He broke through the wall?* Alex thought in horror. That's why Jared had passed out. The amount of energy it must have taken to hold Isic off had taken a toll on him. Jared collapsed onto the steering wheel. The car went out of control. Alicia screamed as Alex grabbed the steering wheel.

"Alicia shift and pull Jared to the back seat!" Alex screamed and tried to get a better handle on the wheel. She shifted and quickly yanked him into the backseat and out of the way. Alex jumped in the driver's seat as Alicia started crying.

"He's unconscious. I can't tell if he's breathing Alex," fear laced her voice. Alex looked in the rearview mirror and saw Isic standing in the middle of the street. He floored it and then went down a hill, losing sight of Isic.

"I'm taking him to the hospital." Alex said breathlessly, driving faster and faster.

"Okay." Alicia said holding Jared in her lap. Alex did a quick glance at Alicia in surprise. He thought for sure she would fight him on this. Pointing out how dangerous it was for them to stop to go to a hospital. Alex guessed the trauma of everything they'd just been through had taken the fight out of her. Alex didn't want to stop, but he knew Jared needed help as soon as possible.

They pulled into the emergency entrance of New York Presbyterian hospital. Alicia ran into the hospital while Alex watched over Jared. It was strange to him not hearing Jared talking. He was breathing, but it was very shallow. Alex didn't want Alicia to see how worried he was. Alex got into the back seat and held Jared's hand. He looked almost peaceful in his unconscious state. Alex hoped Jared wasn't in any pain. Alicia burst out of the emergency doors with two nurses in tow. They pulled a gurney next to the car and gently lifted Jared onto it. Alicia ran into the hospital while Alex parked the car.

Chapter 12

Alex was scared for Jared. He felt responsible for what happened. His plan ended up getting Jared hurt. He grabbed Jared's bag and walked into the hospital. He hung his head in guilt and fatigue. They had rushed Jared into the ICU unit while Alex and Alicia sat in the waiting room. She paced back and forth.

"I know I don't know him, but it feels like I've known him my whole life. It's crazy."

"It's the Awari," Alex said, interrupting her pacing. He filled Alicia in on what he'd learned from Isic.

"That is so fucked up," she stopped pacing and sat down next to Alex. They were silent for a while. Alex looked up and saw a vending machine. He asked Alicia if she wanted anything, she declined. He walked over to the coffee vending machine and brought her some hot chocolate.

"How did you know I liked hot chocolate?" She took a sip.

"I honestly guessed. But I don't know if there's a person alive who doesn't like hot chocolate." He smiled at her, trying to give her comfort.

"I hope he's alright," she whispered taking another sip.

"Me too." Alex sat down and put his arm around her. He closed his eyes and tried to sense if there were any creatures in the building. There were none. He checked the bag to make sure the Awari was still in it. He took it out the bag and held it in his hand. *All of this because of you*, he said to himself. He quickly put it back in the bag.

The doctor came around the corner. He sat down next to them with a perplexed expression on his face. He was hesitant to give them an update because they weren't family. They explained to him that they were Jared's friends and that his parents were out of the country. That seemed to work."It appears your friend had some sort of brain aneurysm."

"Oh, god!" Alicia put the cup down on the table. Alex panicked. He'd never heard of someone surviving an aneurysm before.

"A blood vessel burst in his brain. We were able to stop the bleeding though, and there's been no hemorrhage or neurological damage."

"What are you not telling us?" Alex suspected the doctor was holding something back from them.

"Well, something strange is happening. His entire rupture appears to have been stopped altogether by something that formed over that area. It looks like some kind of synthetic material. I have never seen anything like it." Alex heard himself gulp. He and Alicia exchanged knowing glances while the doctor continued.

"Without that, he would have had a major stroke, or he may have even died." *Jared saved himself by forming a tiny wall over the ruptured area*, Alex thought to himself. A rush of relief flooded his body. That was the best news he'd heard in a very long time. Alicia ran her hands through her hair.

"Can we see him?" The doctor paused.

"Please?" Alicia asked in a sweet voice. She smiled wide making her eyes light up. The older doctor didn't stand a chance against her charm.

"Okay. We're keeping him overnight to run some tests. His brain wave patterns are very unusual." Alex and Alicia knew exactly why that was. They both suspected neither of their brains were the same after gaining powers either. They pressed the call button for the elevator.

"Shit," Alex whispered and looked around the waiting room. He sensed a creature entering the building.

"I know that look Alex." Alicia whispered, following behind the doctor into the elevator.

"There's one headed for Jared. It's taking the stairs."

"This is why I don't like elevators." Alicia said turning around to look at the doctor. The elevator doors opened, and they saw a creature at the end of the hall. The glowing eyes were a dead giveaway. Alex realized all of the patient's rooms were down the hall closer to the creature. He looked at Alicia and she nodded in understanding. They both grabbed the doctor by the arm, and started to speed walk down the hallway.

"What's going on?" The doctor looked at them in alarm.

"Which room is Jared in?" Alex asked, ignoring the doctor's scared look.

"Ro-room seven!" The doctor stuttered as they rushed down the long hallway towards room seven. As they neared Jared's room, Alex noticed one of the guards in the ICU looking at them in a strange way. He quickly put his head down.

"Alicia, I think we have a problem." Alicia looked at the guard staring at them.

"Well, where Is the creature?" she whispered. Alex opened his mouth to answer her when the guard appeared.

"You fit the description of a guy who fled the scene where a cop was killed today." The authority in his voice scared Alex.

"WHAT?" Alicia asked, genuinely shocked.

"I don't know anything about that. I was nowhere near any crime scene today." Alex tried to sound confident, but knew his voice was shaky. He couldn't even give the guard eye contact.

"Wait over here while I call the police." The guard said pulling on Alex's arm.

"We're here to see our friend! We don't know anything about a cop being killed." Alicia raised her voice aggravated. The doctor just stared at them in bewilderment. Alex thought this was probably the weirdest thing the doctor had ever witnessed. First Jared's medical mystery, now two visitors possibly wanted for murdering a cop. Alex's body tensed. He looked at Alicia in fear. She could feel the presence of the creature too.

"Don't shift!" Alex yelled at Alicia, as a man in a white doctor's coat walked towards room seven from the opposite direction. He had red, glowing eyes.

"Fuck! It's going to beat us to Jared's room!" Alex thought for a second as the guard tried to figure out what was happening. He had stopped pulling Alex, but still held onto his arm. *I can't use my powers here and if Alicia changes all hell will break loose,* Alex thought frantically.

Alex slowly started backing up from the guard towards Jared's room.

"Stop or I'll shoot!" The guard changed his stance and pulled out a gun. The doctor's face turned red in anger.

"Are you nuts? There are people on oxygen in here. Are you trying to blow us up?" He screamed at the guard and pulled at his hair. Alex's heart stopped. He had two problems. The guard, and the creature making its way to Jared's room. The nurses and doctors in the unit stopped and stared at the commotion going on.

"FUCK!" Alicia started to run down the hall, as the doctor with the red eyes ran into Jared's room.

"NOOO!" Alex took the risk of getting shot and ran after Alicia. He heard the officer yelling for him to stop, but he kept running. His legs pumped harder and harder until he slid into Jared's room. The creature was on the other side of Jared's bed holding a knife to his unconscious throat. Alicia's skin started changing color as she began to shift. Alex started to power up and then stopped, stunned. A block appeared in front of Jared's bed, pushing the creature backwards full force. It slammed against a wall and slid down to the floor in a heap. Jared was still unconscious, but had conjured up a wall in defense. Alex and Alicia turned their attention back to the creature. The doctor and the guard ran into Jared's room. All eyes landed on the creature. Its red glowing eyes scanned the room, then it scrambled to its feet and dove out of the hospital window. They all rushed to the window and saw the creature land on the roof of a building across the street.

"What the hell just happened?" The guard asked, visibly shaken.

"I don't want to know." The doctor said rubbing his temples. They all looked at the wall around Jared's bed. Alex and Alicia slowly turned their eyes to the guard. It was quiet as they looked to see what he would do next. He looked at Alex, then at the open window the creature had just jumped out of.

"I don't get paid enough for this shit." He holstered his gun and left the room. Alex and Alicia sighed in relief and turned their attention back to Jared. The doctor walked over and started examining him.

"One of us needs to get to Ron asap. Isic told me some of the Awari's powers, but we need to see if Ron can get us more information."

"*One* of us?" Alicia asked looking Alex up and down. Alex readjusted his backpack.

"Yes. One of us has to stay here. We can't leave Jared unguarded in here."
Alicia's eyes got huge, and she pointed to the wall that Jared had put up. She was signifying that Jared could obviously take care of himself.

"I don't want to take any chances Alicia."

"Well, I'll stay. Ron is your friend, not mine," she walked over and sat down next to Jared's bed. Alex nodded okay and gave Jared one last glance before leaving.

"Please be careful," Alicia whispered to Alex as he left the room.

Chapter 13

Alex was beyond tired. He had been running all night. He looked at his watch and saw it was near eleven. He swung Jared's backpack over his shoulder and opened the driver's side door. He started the car and realized the tank was almost on empty.

"Shit!" Alex checked his phone to see how far Ron was from the hospital. It was less than ten miles. He decided he could make it there without having to stop for gas. He pulled up his contacts and dialed Ron.

"Hey man! Where are you? I've been sitting here all day." Alex apologized and started driving faster. He was doing scans as he drove. The drive to NYU was the first quiet moments he'd had to himself in a long time. He started thinking about Daniel. He started to reminisce about their time together when a car honked its horn at him. He had been driving too close to the other side of the road. He snapped out of his trance and felt the backpack, making sure the Awari was still in it.

He reached NYU and called Ron again. He was one of the smartest people Alex knew and he trusted him completely. They hugged and Alex took his backpack off.

"Let's see whatcha got here," Ron pointed to the backpack. Alex noticed how excited Ron was to see the Awari.

"It's safer if I show you inside," Alex warned Ron, doing another scan of the area. Ron agreed and they walked up the steps to the door. Ron slid a keycard into the door and led them down a long hallway.

"I hope you don't mind, but I asked a friend of mine to meet us here." Alex's steps faltered slightly. He didn't want to put anyone else in danger, and he wasn't sure who he could trust.

"You trust him?" Alex asked, voicing his inner thoughts.

"More than most people, yes." Ron said with confidence.

"He's a researcher at the center for Latin American and Caribbean studies. I just thought he may have some ideas about this. He studied a tablet of writing that may be related to the Awari." Although Alex was still somewhat skeptical, he trusted Ron. There were various reproductions of famous artwork on the building's walls as they walked through another set of large double doors. These doors were very thick and looked very strong. Alex watched Ron punch in a code, then he slid his keycard into a grey slot on the side of the door.

"Here we are," Ron opened his arms wide as they walked in.

There were a variety of machines and equipment. It was the brightest room Alex had ever seen. There was a very large table in the middle of the room with cameras and robotic arms overhead. On the sides of the walls were small rods with lenses. There were also rows and rows of test tubes sitting on very large shelves. There was another room on the other side of this room. Alex could tell Ron enjoyed his work because his voice went up three octaves talking about it. Ron led him into a control room located on the other side of the room. He motioned for Alex to come in. Ron pushed a few buttons to turn the lights out in the main room they had just left. There were monitors built into the control panel. There were so many lights flashing and blinking that they reminded Alex of Christmas.

"I thought we could gather more information by further scrutinizing the idol. It's common knowledge in the scientific community, that a large ancient stone was located by Cornell University. The stone is from an area in Mexico. They called it the Awari stone." Alex's heart rate sped up. He was laser focused on every word Ron was saying. Finally, he could get the answers they needed. They walked out of the control room and Ron turned the lights back on in the main research lab.

"That team mapped the ancient stone's origin and discovered that there were ancient inscriptions on the stone that were previously missed."

"How did they do that?" Alex asked out of curiosity. He adjusted the backpack.

"Using an x-ray fluorescence imaging system," Ron said like it was something Alex should have already known.

"The machine is a million times stronger than a medical imaging machine. My friend Timo has a deep interest in epigraphy and is very familiar with the Awari stone."

"What's epi…whatever you just said," Alex asked in confusion. Ron chuckled, realizing he wasn't talking to someone with his scientific knowledge.

"Sorry. Epigraphy is the study of incised writing on various surfaces, including stone." Alex nodded his understanding even though he didn't understand it at all. There was a ringing noise and they both looked towards a desk on the other side of the room.

"Excuse me for a second Alex." While Ron was on his phone, Alex checked his phone for messages. He texted Alicia, asking about Jared's condition.

"Timo is outside. I need to walk down and get him. You can wait here." Alex looked around the room full of things he did not understand. His phone vibrated. Alicia had sent him a picture of Jared.

"Whoa!" Alex said into the empty room. Jared had completely enclosed himself within his wall. Alicia texted back that the doctors are trying to figure out how this is happening. He texted her, play *dumb*. She quickly responded, *no prob*.

Ron walked back in the room with a very short man. He looked to be in his mid-thirties. He had dark hair that completely covered his forehead. He had on a research jacket. His thin mustache did not match his baby face. Timo walked directly up to Alex and shook his hand.

"Ron told me that you have the Awari." Alex gently took the Awari from the backpack.

"My god! I can't believe you were able to buy something like this from a street vendor." Timo reached for it, but Alex pulled it back. Timo gave Alex a surprised look.

"I would like to see it please." Alex hesitated. He still had reservations about trusting him. He looked over at Ron, who gave him a nod. Alex relaxed a little and held it out towards Timo, but didn't give it to him. Timo squealed in delight, causing Alex to jump back in shock.

"I'm sorry. It's just so rare to see such history up close and personal," Timo and Ron's excitement rose. Timo's eyes gleamed as he reached for the Awari. Alex pulled it back again.

"It's best that you don't touch it. Crazy things happen to the people who touch it. Trust me, it's for your own safety." Timo looked even more intrigued and stepped back. He motioned for Alex to put the Awari on a table underneath a light. The three of them went into the control room. Ron hit a button and the lights went off in the main room. The Awari started glowing a faint blue color. Timo and Ron started pushing various buttons. The rods on the sides of the room glowed, and bright lights flashed out of their tips towards the Awari. After about thirty minutes of this, Alex sat down while Ron and Timo continued to examine the Awari. An hour later, they exited the control room. Timo and Ron were holding sheets of paper.

"The Awari you have is real." Timo said with certainty. *No shit*, Alex thought sarcastically.

"Do you have any idea what this means?" Alex shrugged in confusion.

"No, that's why I'm here," Alex was trying to keep the annoyance out of his voice. He wished they would just get to the point.

"No one thought the legend of the Awari was real. We just tested the age of the Awari, and it's old. Ancient. But we just discovered something that wasn't

143

previously documented. The Awari is putting out an electrical charge." Timo leaned in close to Alex like he was sharing a secret.

"Picture spark plugs on a car that can generate its own energy. That's what the Awari is doing. Generating its own energy." Timo and Ron shared a look.

"What was that look for?" Alex asked in apprehension. Timo walked to the control panel.

"The Awari is said to have come from an ancient race of aliens." Alex remembered what Alicia told him in Jared's apartment, and the crazy things Isic had said. The dots were slowly, but surely, connecting for him. Timo looked down at the papers in his hands.

"The x-ray is showing a sort of wiring within the idol. The tests of the outside of the Awari prove its ancient, so how the hell can there be wiring inside of it? The technology capable of doing that would not have been around in ancient times. Unless it was alien tech. There are no breaks in the outside structure, which also proves to me that an advanced alien tech created this thing."

"These findings are huge! The scientific community must know about it." Ron exclaimed, writing notes down. Alex started to panic.

No one could or should know anything about this evil statue, Alex thought in fear.

"We can't! Not yet. Please keep this between us for now." Alex pleaded with the two researchers who were brimming with excitement.

"Timo, Ron told me you studied the research of some sort of tablet related to the Awari. What did it say?" Alex asked, trying to change the subject. He wanted to know about the writings, but he also wanted Ron and Timo to forget about trying to expose the Awari to the world. Timo's eyes lit up at the subject of the tablet.

144

"It talked of a god named Acan." Alex took a deep breath at the mention of Acan's name.

"Acan was the son of a very powerful man." *Isic,* Alex thought with rage. He shook his head clear of his anger towards Isic and concentrated on Timo.

"A lot of what was written was damaged, but I pieced together what was salvageable. From what I could gather, the world they lived in was populated by very powerful beings. Aliens we now know. These aliens had all kinds of powers and special abilities. They could tap into one hundred percent of their brain's capacity at once, giving them abilities that we could only dream of. Some could create food out of thin air, some could become invisible. Some could even fly. The people on that planet battled each other to see who was the strongest. The tablet suggested that Acan was the king of his people. It said he had the power to harness the sun itself." Alex thought about his powers. The fire and explosions he was able to conjure came from the sun. Just like Acan's. Isic was right about him having Acan's powers.

"He was married to a woman who also had special abilities. Somehow his wife's powers started to wane. They panicked because of the implications of not having any special abilities. Anyone without abilities were looked at as being handicapped or weak. The unpowered people were cast out. There is a mention of them being banished from their world."

Alex's eyes were glued to Timo. This all seemed so familiar and yet so strange. It was as if a part of him knew all of this.

"Acan loved this woman very deeply and he did not want to lose her. The story is that he spoke to this powerful man, his father, who had the power to create things. Acan begged his father to create something that would give his wife the ability to use her powers again. The Awari was created for her. Her name was Itzel. But his father betrayed him and told their people that the only reason she could use her powers

145

was because of the Awari. He wanted to be king himself and needed to find a way to remove Acan. What better way than to make a king choose between his people and his wife? But his betrayal backfired on him when the council found out he created the Awari. They punished him by stripping him of his powers. He went mad. He tried again and again to create another Awari and was never successful again. At some point, he stole the Awari. He kidnapped and sacrificed people to try to get power from the Awari in a bloody ceremony at a temple." Alex remembered that scene like he was there. Ron stood up. He had taken a seat as Timo was talking.

"Man, this sounds like some crazy science fiction story." Alex laughed, because it did sound ridiculous. But it was all real. That made him sober up quick. His phone rang. It was Alicia.

"I need to take this." Alex walked towards the corner of the room.

"Is everything okay?"

"Everything is okay with Jared. He's enclosed in his walls. The doctors and police have tried to move it, it won't budge. He's safer than you and me at the moment." Alex breathed a sigh of relief.

"I found out something that we need to talk about in person. Can you meet me in Central park?" Alex thought her voice sounded strained.

"Sure. But why Central park of all places?" Alex got a bad feeling about this. Something was off with Alicia.

"My dad used to take me there when I was little. It's the one place in New York that makes me feel safe." Alex didn't understand that logic, but he went with it. Alicia kept talking in a rushed voice.

"I think I know why the leader wants the Awari so bad. I need to talk to you about this in person." Alex didn't know why Alicia couldn't just tell him over the phone. She was acting very strange. More strange than usual. He told Alicia he would

146

meet her at three a.m. She mumbled a thank you and hung up. Alex carefully picked up the Awari off of the research table and put it back into the bag.

"Thank you so much for helping me guys." Alex zipped the backpack and secured it on his shoulders.

"No problem, man." Timo shook his hand and Ron gave him a hug.

"Bring back the Awari when you're done. Man, we're going to be famous for finding that thing!" Alex rolled his eyes as Ron walked him out of the research room.

Chapter 14

Alex had just enough gas to make it the few miles to Central Park from NYU. He pulled up with three minutes to spare. He had never been to the park at this time of day before. He'd always considered it a beautiful calm place whenever he visited there. He started to walk around the park, but didn't see Alicia anywhere. A very strange feeling came over him. A foreboding feeling that something was wrong. He reached out with his senses to try to do a scan of her, but couldn't find her.

Could she have been attacked walking here? Alex asked himself, suddenly worried for Alicia's wellbeing. He hesitantly walked deeper into the park. It was still dark out. He called out Alicia's name. She suddenly appeared from around a corner.

"Hey! Why didn't I sense you?" He asked her, running up to give her a hug. He remembered that he couldn't get a good sense of her at Jared's apartment either. He noticed she wasn't hugging him back. As Alex released her, he noticed a man walking around the same corner Alicia had just come from.

"Oh my god!" It was Isic. Alex backed up from Alicia, who had yet to say anything since rounding that corner.

"What the hell is going on?" Alicia's eyes were watering.

"Please Alex, he has my brother." Alicia's voice cracked with emotion and terror. Alex's skin started to tingle as he saw twenty pairs of red eyes looking at him.

"Alicia! How could you?"

"Alex he will kill my brother if you don't give him the Awari!" Alicia screamed in agony as tears fell down her cheeks. She looked like she was in physical pain. Alex didn't know much about Alicia, but he knew that Isic would indeed kill her brother. As much as it pained him to make her choose, Alex just couldn't give Isic the Awari.

"We can't Alicia. You know what this thing will do if he joins the Awari's together." Alex's heart ached looking at Alicia's desperate face.

"It will be the end for everyone." Alicia walked up to Alex still crying.

"Alex, please don't make me take It from you." Alex's blood turned cold at her threat. He knew he wasn't strong enough to fight Alicia. He hoped it didn't come down to that. He looked over at Isic, who had a smug look on his face. He was enjoying this.

"You would try to take it from me Alicia?" Alex asked in sad shock. He couldn't blame her though. She was in a no-win situation.

"I will do ANYTHING for my brother," Alicia pointed behind her. Alex looked at what she was pointing at and almost fainted. Isic had a sickle up to the neck of a young boy. He was about twelve years old. He had on pajamas and a look of terror on his face.

"Oh, god. I—I can't, Alicia. I'm sorry!" Alicia took a deep breath and stopped crying. She was angry now. Alex started to back away from her. Alex caught movement out of the corner of his eye. Isic had gestured for more creatures to assemble. Alex hadn't even sensed their presence. He looked over at Alicia in a panic. She arched her brow at him. Alex realized immediately why he hadn't sensed her or the creatures.

"You have the ability to block other people's powers, don't you?" It came out more as an accusation than a question.

"I didn't know if I could trust you enough to tell you the full extent of what I could do." Alex thought about the time her hair had turned to needles to kill that creature in the parking garage. She had claimed it was a new power. She had been lying all along about what she could do and how powerful she was.

"But I sensed you in Jared's building."

"I let you know I was there." Alicia admitted looking him in the eyes.

"What else are you not telling me, Alicia?" She broke eye contact with him and started to cry again. Isic moved forward with Alicia's brother. He gave the sickle to one of the creatures, and wrapped his hand around the little boy's neck.

"Please don't!" Alicia reached out towards her brother, then pulled back as Isic let her brother go. In a split second, he pushed the boy into one of his creatures.

"Acan, you can't win. Do you want to be responsible for the death of this little boy?" Alex watched the creature hover over Alicia's brother. Alicia wrung her wrists in nervousness.

"Shame on you Acan." Isic shook his finger at Alex and sucked his teeth.

Alex hated this. He turned to Alicia in defeat.

"I won't do it, Alicia. I won't." Alicia sighed and started to shift.

"Then you leave me no choice." Alex started to power up, but nothing happened. Alicia was blocking his powers. Alicia ran towards him. He was shocked at how fast she was. Alex concentrated as hard as he could to power up. Alicia was

150

strong, but he had the power of the sun. He had to focus to harness that power. Alicia slowed down as light started emitting from Alex's body. They locked eyes as Alex released it in her direction. The light blinded her, making her grab at her eyes. Alex ran in the opposite direction while he had the chance. Blinded, Alicia ran into a park bench, tripping and falling into the grass.

"Very good, Acan. I see you are learning to use your power in more creative ways. Which means I need to end this quickly." Isic looked over at Alicia laying on the ground. She grunted in frustration and got up.

"Give me the goddamned bag, Alex! I don't want to hurt you, but I will." Alex didn't budge. He knew he might die tonight, but he felt it was worth it to keep the Awari out of Isic's hands. Alicia reached over and grabbed a tree. Alex watched in shock as she ripped it out of the ground. He could hear the roots snapping as she picked it up and held it like a battering ram. Alex concentrated on locking a symbol onto Alicia. She was exerting so much energy, it was getting easier to call upon his powers. She started running towards Alex. He had a symbol locked onto her. He didn't want to hurt her, but he had to do something to slow her down. She ran towards him then at the last second changed directions. Alex lost his concentration at her sudden misdirection.

"What the fuck?"

"I know what you are trying to do," she said, running in a jagged direction. Alex tried to lock back on her again, but she kept zigzagging. It was damned near impossible. He followed her, but she was so fast. He blinked and then she was gone. Alex searched the area and tried to sense her. He felt something near him but couldn't tell what it was. He heard rustling leaves and looked up. She was in a tree above him and was jumping down from above him. Adrenaline and fear kicked in and Alex focused on the tree. It immediately exploded and split in two. Alicia came flying through the splintered tree, landing right in front of Alex like a cat. She picked him up and threw him across the park like he weighed nothing.

"WHOA!" Alex screamed as he flailed through the air. He landed hard in a patch of grass, the wind was knocked out of him. He looked up from the ground at Alicia. He was still in shock that she'd just attacked him like that. She picked up another tree and started to swing it like a bat. Alex tried to catch his breath. His body was hurting everywhere. He looked over at Isic, who was clearly enjoying this. His eyes were lit up with glee.

"This reminds me of the good old days on our home world, Acan. Does it not?" He thought about Timo saying the people on that world battled each other to see who was the strongest.

"Alex, give me the fucking bag!" Alicia screamed through clenched teeth, holding the tree at her side. Alex ignored the pain that was radiating through his body and scanned the park. He could see wires and pipes underground. There were large pools of water that looked like small lakes underneath them. Alicia slowly walked towards Alex.

"Please, Alex." Alicia looked exhausted and stressed. Alex closed his eyes and focused on the pipes below the park.

"Stop right there, Alicia." Alex pushed himself to his feet. He put his hands up in a defensive stance. She stopped.

"What are you going to do? Focus on blowing me up like you tried to do to those things in the garage?" Alicia actually looked hurt. Alex didn't respond right away. He had locked symbols on a large pipe.

"You wouldn't hurt me, would you, Alex?" Alicia's hurt voice went in one ear and out of the other. Alex closed his eyes again. He could hear Isic yelling something at Alicia. He told her to kill Alex. Alex knew he had little time, so he released the energy he had been building. He focused on the pipes directly under Alicia and Isic. Before Alicia could react, the ground exploded and the ground beneath them catapulted them both back fifty feet. Alicia landed on her feet, but Isic fell to his.

"Smart boy," Isic sounded impressed. Alicia's little brother screamed.

"Ally!" Alex could see him trying to struggle to get free of the creatures. One of them scratched his face with the sickle and told him to shut up. Alex was so tired. He was having a hard time focusing on his next move. Alicia got up and immediately shifted. In her shifted form, Alex couldn't tell if she was hurt by the explosion. Alicia's little brother struggled again to get free. Creatures started surrounding Alex. One of them swiftly punched him in the face, knocking him to the ground.

"FUCK!" Alex screamed out in pain as another one kicked him in the side. He laid on the ground defenseless as Isic walked up to him. He looked down with an evil grin. The same one he'd shown Acan, before killing Itzel. Alicia stood off to the side, waiting. Her eyes never left her brother.

"Get the Awari then kill him now! Your brother will go free." Isic smiled at her, showing his teeth. Alicia quickly looked at Alex, seemingly deciding what to do. "Don't believe him, Alicia!" Alex yelled, trying to stay steady on his feet.

"He's going to kill us all if you do!" Alicia looked directly at Alex. It still amazed Alex how alien she looked in this state. She moved so quick, and was in front of Alex before he could do anything to stop her. She lifted him up by his wrists easily. Alex couldn't fight back. His body was so exhausted, it felt like it was shutting down on him. He tried to pull on his dwindling powers. She looked him directly in the eyes. Her features were completely dark except for her glowing eyes. Alex could tell she was crying. She was making whimpering sounds. His stomach dropped as he watched her hair start growing out of her scalp. He knew what was coming next.

"I'm so sorry, Alex." Her muffled voice was full of sadness. The hair wrapped around Alex's arms. The strands started to harden. Alex took in a sharp breath. The pain took him by surprise. Thin needles started forming out of the strands, slowly penetrating into Alex's skin.

"OH GOD! ALICIA STOP!" Alex's agonized screamed echoed through the park. Through his painful, blurry vision, Alex saw Isic pick up the backpack. A creepy smile spread across his face, as he moved his hands throughout the backpack. Alex closed his eyes and realized he was about to die. He could feel Alicia's needles at his throat. Alex was in so much pain, but he was also at peace. *I can finally be with Daniel.* That thought ran through Alex's mind as the needles dug deeper and deeper into his skin.

"The Awari is not in here! ACAN!" Isic furiously screamed out.

"What?" Alicia loosened her grip on Alex.

"It is not in here, you stupid bitch! Can't you hear? There is nothing in here but a big fucking rock!" Isic threw the bag down on the ground and stormed over to Alex. He reached up and put his hands around Alex's face, squishing his jaw.

"If you don't tell me where it is right now, I will rip your fucking eyes out." The venomous look in Isic's eyes were frightening. Alex looked at Isic in defiance and stayed quiet.

"Wait! I know where it is." Alicia put Alex down and turned towards Isic. Alex collapsed to the ground, and looked at Alicia in confusion.

"Another power?" Alex guessed immediately looking at Alicia. She nodded her head yes.

I can see who you were in the past. But I can also see what you did in the past. That includes the last hour." Alex watched in defeat as Alicia's eyes started to glow.

"Please, Alicia, don't!" Alex whispered to Alicia.

"I have no choice, Alex. My brother is only twelve years old." She cried and closed her eyes.

"Well? Where is it, bitch? I don't have all night!" Isic yelled in impatience, walking next to her.

"It's under a small blanket near the bushes a few feet away. Alex hid the Awari there before meeting us." Alicia opened her eyes and looked at Alex in shame. She wasn't proud of what she'd just done. Alex had a bad feeling as soon as he had walked into the park. He'd hid the Awari just in case he got attacked. Tears fell down Alex's cheek as he looked at Alicia. He was so angry, yet he couldn't blame her.

"Get it now and bring it to me!" Isic commanded. Alicia ran off. Isic stood directly in front of Alex.

"Finally, this will be over. I can't wait to kill that bitch and her little brother. Those souls will help feed my power even more! But you Acan, I want to make you suffer before the Awari absorbs your soul." Isic bent down and smacked Alex in the face. He grimaced in pain at the attack. He thought about him blowing to pieces, but he was so weak. Even if he could, he needed time to focus and get Alicia and her brother out of harm's way.

Alicia called out to Isic. She stood about twenty feet away.

"Let my brother go now and the Awari is yours." Alicia held it up to show Isic she did indeed have it.

"Are you trying to bargain with me?" Isic asked incredulously.

"I can create an army of creatures that will rip you limb from limb!"

"I will fucking destroy this thing if you don't let him go right now! Let him go and I will give it to you. That's the deal." Alicia had a deadly look in her eyes. Isic stayed quiet for a minute, then signaled for the creatures to bring her brother forward. Alicia looked so relieved. Alex could see the love she had for her brother.

155

"Okay, asshole. On the count of three, you let him go and I will throw you the Awari." Isic mumbled something that sounded like, "whatever, bitch," and nodded.

"One…" Alicia held up the Awari.

"Two…" Alex thought about trying to blow the Awari up, but thought about all of the souls trapped inside it.

"Three!" Alicia's little brother ran from the pack of creatures. Alicia bit her bottom lip and threw the Awari. It flew through the air in what felt like slow motion. Isic licked his lips in anticipation. The Awari was still flying through the air when Alicia wrapped her arms around her brother. Alex looked closer at the Awari. Small squares started to form around it. *What the hell?* Alex thought to himself, thinking he was hallucinating. Alex kept his eyes on the Awari. It was now completely enclosed in what looked like a stone box. Alicia shifted back as the Awari fell to the ground. Her little brother held on to her tight. Isic's eyes were just as baffled as Alex's. He took a step closer to the box the Awari had been encased in. The box suddenly flew from the ground and directly into Jared's hands.

Chapter 15

"It's amazing what a nap can do for the body." Jared smiled and winked at Alex. Alex didn't have much time to digest Jared's presence, before Isic made a whistling sound. Suddenly, creatures started running towards Jared. He created more blocks than Alex could keep his eyes on. They were everywhere. Just as quickly as he made them, he changed them into arrows. Each arrow picked a creature to target. One by one, each arrow found its mark. Jared held on tight to the box housing the Awari. Isic's eyes glowed bright red. The creatures that were near Alex rushed towards Jared. *He can't keep this up all night*, Alex thought with worry. Alicia sat on her knees on the ground, holding her brother who was shaking with fear. Jared shot more arrows at the creatures. Just as they died, it seemed ten more came to take their place. He formed a huge wall that knocked them back. Alex was impressed. More and more creatures started coming from every direction of the park. Alex could sense them again. Alicia had stopped blocking him. Alex called out to Jared.

"We can't stop them all like this." Isic seemed to be in a trance, as he watched creature by creature get massacred by Jared's arrows. The creatures kept coming. Alex realized Isic must have called every creature in New York that he'd ever created. Alex could feel them coming from different directions of the city. Jared acknowledged what Alex said and ran towards Alicia and her brother. He killed creature after creature in the process. Jared stopped in front of Alicia and closed his eyes. He crouched down and held onto Alicia and her brother. Alex's strength was waning, but he was able to count at least two hundred creatures entering the park. The creatures surrounded Isic, protecting him. Alex tried again to lock onto Isic, but couldn't. Alex took a deep breath and ran towards Alicia, her brother, and Jared. Creatures chased Alex, but Jared held them at bay, launching arrows in every direction.

"Are you both okay?" Alex asked softly, kneeling down towards Alicia and her brother. Alicia was crying. Alex could see she was visibly tired.

"I am so sorry, Alex. I didn't know what else to do." Alicia cried and wrapped her arms around Alex's neck. He held her tight, consoling her.

"It's okay. I should never have made you choose." Alex felt his own tears starting to fall. Jared looked at them and then back at a barrage of creatures headed towards them.

"We need to figure something out and fast!" Alicia let go of Alex and cleared her nose. She looked up at Jared and her eyes glazed over like she was remembering something.

"I could see into his past. He has a crippling fear of fire. It's one of the reasons he hates you so much. The power you get from the sun scares him. It's the only thing that can kill him." Alex tried to think of how that could help them. He had only used his power for explosions before.

"You can't blow him up, but you can burn the fucker alive." Alicia said hugging her brother again. Alex thought back to the scene at the temple.

"Oh, shit! Acan killed Isic that way, by burning him alive. Well he would have, if the Awari hadn't absorbed his soul." Jared looked over his shoulder at Alex.

"Well, buddy, looks like you have work to do." Alex panicked. He was so tired and exhausted. He didn't think he could stand straight, let alone power up. He put on a brave face and took a few steps away from Jared and Alicia. He closed his eyes and tried to conjure as much power as he could. Jared formed an enclosure around them. Jared raised his hands to the sky and formed blocks above them. Then Jared brought his hands to his sides and created blocks on the left and right of them. He had formed a giant dome. Isic yelled out a command to his creatures. Alex opened his eyes and saw at least one hundred creatures racing towards them. A ray of sun gleamed into his eyes. The sun was coming up. *The sun! I have the power of the sun!* Alex thought quickly as he raised his arms to the sky. He closed his eyes and let the heat and fire of the rising sun fill his body. He felt strength and power like he'd never known. He looked down at himself and realized he was glowing a bright yellow.

"WHOA! Alex, you're on fire!" Alex heard Jared scream as he realized he indeed was on fire. But he felt no heat. He had no burns. He just felt powerful and strong. Alex focused on the creatures running towards them and easily focused and blew them apart. Isic and the creatures started to realize that Jared was trapping them inside of the dome he was creating. Some creatures ran, but about fifty were trapped as Jared fully closed them off from the rest of the park. Alex looked at the dome in amazement. Alex felt the rush of the sun's power running through his veins. He started to power up again. This time he let the energy keep building instead of releasing it. Isic looked at him in horror. Alex started to glow. He clenched his fists and breathed. He felt as if he had done this before. The spirit of Acan was flowing through him. Creatures were frantically pounding on the walls of the dome to get out. Isic ran towards the dome and started punching the walls. Alex could see Jared clenching his teeth and closing his eyes. Alex didn't want a repeat of what happened to Jared the last time Isic was able to break free from one of his walls.

"Enough of this! ISIC!" Alex yelled out. Isic stood erect and turned around. Alex looked at Isic as Isic sized him up. *If I kill him, I lose any chance of getting Daniel back. But I have no choice. He will destroy this world if we don't stop him.* Alex convinced himself that there was only one thing to do. Alex tapped into some of the energy he'd been holding onto, and released it. Waves of energy, flames, and light shot from his body. It hit Isic full blast, throwing him hard against the dome walls. Alex turned his focus on the creatures still inside the dome. He concentrated on turning his explosion into fire. He locked a symbol on each creature, then let loose a blast of flames. Isic's creatures screamed as they caught fire. Alex felt more power rushing through his body. He released a second wave of flames near Isic. The grass started to burn. He watched the trees within the dome catch fire. Isic tried to get off the ground before the flames from the grass caught up to him. He was too slow. The piercing scream that left his throat made each of them shudder. Fully ablaze, Isic started walking towards Alex. His burning figure took three steps then he fell on his knees. His skin was starting to peel off. Alex looked at Alicia who looked terrified. She held on tight to her brother and shielded his eyes. Alex watched Isic burn and thought about Daniel. He smiled and closed his eyes.

"Daniel, this is for you" Alex released the rest of the power waiting to get out. Another wave of fire and light rippled across the grass, and onto Isic. Isic had stopped screaming and was now whimpering in pain. He put both of his hands up in front of his face. He made another attempt to stand up as more fire enveloped him. Parts of his skin fell off. His burning body collapsed and fell to the ground. They all watched in silence as Isic's body burned down to his skeleton. Alex walked over and stomped on Isic's charred skull. He could feel the creatures start to disappear and disintegrate all over the city. All at once they were gone. Alex pulled the flames back into his body and collapsed on the ground. He was truly and utterly maxed out. He laid on his back looking at the ceiling of the dome.

"We did it, Daniel." Jared's dome started to fade away. Alicia ran over to Alex and started crying. She bent down wrapping her arms around him. He contently held her tight.

"It's okay now. It's over."

Epilogue

Alex looked out of the window at the clouds. It was the first time in a long time that he could actually appreciate their beauty. Seeing the world from this height gave him a feeling that was out of this world. The sun light was a distant haze. He smiled to himself, thinking about Daniel. He wanted to remember the good times they had together. Even when they had been at their worst, the memory was still a great one. He shifted in the seat and took a sip of his orange juice. He could hear Alicia arguing with Jared about who had better fashion sense. Jared ran up to his seat fast, startling him. He started talking so fast that Alex laughed and told him to take a breath.

"How in the world do you both have so much energy this early?" Alex asked, pushing Jared back a little. Jared laughed and rolled his eyes.

"Well, to quote Rick James, 'cocaine is a hell of a drug'", Jared started cracking up. Alex made a disapproving sound and looked at Jared sideways.

"I hope you're kidding."

"I am!" he said laughing.

"I'm high on life. Can't you tell?" He said with a big grin on his face. Alex put his orange juice down.

"It's easy to be high on life when you're rich." Alex got comfortable in his seat.

"That's not my fault. This is my parents' money. I was just born into it. I used to hate it, but it is nice that they let us use their private jet to fly to Mexico right?" Alex shook his head in agreement.

"Hell yeah!" He high fived Jared and they both laughed. Alex turned back to see Alicia playing a game on her phone. Ron and Timo both were nose deep in their papers and research books. Jared sat down next to Alex, and leaned over towards him.

"Aren't you even a little nervous about what we might find in there?" Alex turned towards Jared and thought for a second.

"I am. But in some strange way, it feels as if I'm returning home." Jared looked out of the window.

"It feels that way for me too, but I'm still a little nervous." The minute the doors opened to the plane, Alicia yelled out.

"Oh, shit! It's hot as hell out here!"

"Welcome to Mexico." Alex said to her while walking down the steps. Timo and Ron had hired two drivers to take them out to the approximate location of the temple. Timo said that natives and tourists stayed away from that location. It was so far off the main roads, they didn't think it was safe. They had rented RV's and got busy loading them up. After driving for a while, they decided to take naps.

"We should be there by the morning," Alex said to Alicia after reading their map again.

"I never thought I would leave the country." Alicia looked out the window in awe.

"How does it feel?"

"It feels good," she smiled and settled into a lying position next to Alex. They left around three a.m. Timo and Ron were in the RV behind them with their equipment. The roads became rockier and rougher as they got closer. Some of the roads had rivers running right through them. They drove on a road that was on the side of a cliff with rocks falling down. It reminded them that they were far from civilization. Alex heard Timo on the radio, "we're here!" His voice was full of excitement. The RV stopped. Alicia jumped up and slid the doors open. Alex stepped out of the RV and could not believe his eyes at the familiarity of the temple. It was the shape of a pyramid, but had a huge statue standing in front of it. The statue was about a hundred feet tall. It was an exact replica of the Awari. Timo practically ran from the RV and started taking pictures.

"I can't believe this," Timo kept repeating that over and over as he clicked away.

Jared got out of the RV and yawned.

"Don't forget we're the reason you found it." Between Alex, Jared, and Alicia's connection to the Awari, they were able to pinpoint exactly where the temple was on the map. It was as if they just knew. Like it was home. Ron pulled out a metal briefcase. Inside was the Awari idol. Ron opened the case and turned it towards Alex. He picked it up as Jared and Alicia walked over to him. It felt warm in his hands and started to glow. As soon as he held it, he had a sense that it needed to go into the temple. They all walked under the legs of the giant Awari statue into the temple. Timo turned on the giant flashlights he'd brought with him. There were burn marks all over the walls. They slowly walked down the temple steps. Large pillars blocked their path. Thanks to Alicia, they were able to move them. They eventually reached the ceremonial room. Jared looked at Alex. He seemed nervous.

"Doesn't this feel familiar to you?" Alex and Alicia looked at Jared and nodded in unison.

"Yes. It feels like we're supposed to be here, at this moment."

"I feel like that too," Alicia chimed in. They walked into the middle of the room. The Awari started to glow all of a sudden. The light was so bright, they had to shield their eyes. Alex set the Awari on the ground, then they all backed up. Timo started taking pictures again. Alicia grabbed Alex's hand and reached for Jared's. Once their hands were joined, they watched as the Awari idol pulsed blue and white. The lights flashed and then it turned back to blue. A ray of blue light shot out of it and into the wall on the other side of the room.

"Holy shit!" Jared exclaimed as Alicia shrieked in surprise. They all laughed nervously and looked around the temple. Alex noticed for the first time that there were skeletons laying against the temple walls. He said a silent prayer for the deceased victims of Isic. He started to walk over to a wall. He put his hand up to it. It was very warm.

"There's something on the other side of this wall. Alicia, can you help me for a second?" She started shifting.

"That is so cool!" Timo watched in fascination as Alicia turned all black. Alex used his power and saw the other idol on the other side of that wall. In the blueprint in his mind, he found the weakest point of the wall.

"Punch right here." She retracted her arm and hit the wall.

"Jared, as soon as I say the word, form a box around the second idol." Jared walked over to the wall and closed his eyes. The wall crumbled under the force of Alicia's punch. Jared formed a square to hold the top of the wall steady as Alex reached for the second idol. As soon as Alex pulled it through the hole, the original Awari shot a beam of light directly into it.

"The Awari is controlled by the intention of the person wielding it. Isic's intentions weren't pure, so the Awari became an instrument of death and destruction. In the right hands, you could turn it into a tool for good." Alicia recited.

"How do you know that?" Jared's surprised voice echoed throughout the temple.

"When I touched the Awari, I felt that it wasn't meant to be used for what Isic turned it into."

"Okay, so what now?" Alex was holding the second idol like it was an egg. Alicia walked over to him and talked softly to him.

"Think about what you want it to do, Alex. It's all about your intentions." Jared and Alicia moved back to where Ron and Timo were standing. Alex took a deep breath and slowly walked to the center of the room. The second idol got warmer and warmer the closer it got to the Awari. Alex bent down and carefully connected the two idols. The eyes of the idols started to pulse blue.

"Oh shit!" Alex stepped back and stood next to Jared. The floor started vibrating.

"What's happening?" Alicia asked trying to keep her balance.

"I'm not sure." Jared almost tipped over as the vibrations got stronger.

"What did you tell the Awari to do Alex? Bring the place down?" Alicia fell backwards as the floor shook even harder. Alex grabbed onto a pillar to steady himself.

"I told it to release the innocent souls trapped inside of it." A beam of light shot straight up from the center of the joined idols. It's force punched a hole through the temple ceiling. Dust filled the ceremonial room. A soft white light came out of the idols. It pulsed like a heartbeat. Alex looked around the temple. Alicia was speechless. Timo took pictures. Ron was furiously writing notes and hitting buttons on his equipment. Shapes started forming all around the room. The dust in the room swirled slightly. Alex noticed a hand, then an arm. A second later a body stood in front of the group. It was Daniel. Alex's breath left his body as his knees started to give out.

"Daniel?" His voice cracked at seeing Daniel bathed in the soft light. Jared and Alicia gasped. Alex thought he was dreaming. He timidly walked over to Daniel, hoping he wasn't a mirage. His heart was beating a million beats per second. He felt faint. He didn't want to cry and tried so hard not to. He put his hand out towards Daniel's form, scared to touch him. Daniel smiled at him lovingly.

"I missed you." Daniel reached his right arm out to Alex.

"I missed you, too. Oh god, so much." Alex broke down. Tears started rolling down his face. He felt Daniel's soft hand wiping the tears off his cheek.

"How is this possible, Daniel?"

"You wished to see me one last time." After Alex told the Awari to release the innocent souls, he did make a wish to see Daniel one more time.

"Does it hurt?" Alex asked looking at Daniel from head to toe. Daniel looked at his body.

"Not at all." Daniel looked over Alex's shoulder at Alicia and smiled at her. Alicia tearfully smiled back. Alex walked closer to Daniel.

"I don't know how I can live this life without you. You're my soul mate." Alex started to cry again.

"You will live and prosper, Alex. And I'll never leave you. Look at me," Daniel put his finger under Alex's chin.

"Your work is not done. You will be and are needed."

"What do you mean?" Alex grabbed and held Daniel's hands. Daniel smiled at their joined hands.

"You'll see. Great things are in store for you." Alex nodded although he didn't fully understand.

"Can I hug you one last time?" Alex asked desperately. Daniel opened his arms. Alex walked closer to him.

"There's nothing I want more," Daniel said and reached out for Alex. Alex wrapped his arms around Daniel. As soon as their bodies touched, all of the memories of their time together flooded Alex's mind. It was a warm, comforting feeling. All of the happiness he'd lost since Daniel's death came back full force. Daniel put his hand on Alex's face.

"I love you. Always." Daniel's form started to fade.

"Please don't leave me," Alex pleaded as Daniel smiled at him. A second later he was gone. Another flash of light shot out of the idols. The light hit the walls in the room. People bathed in soft lights started appearing and walking out of the center of the light. Many of the souls smiled as they walked past the group. Some flew straight up into the air. Others looked a little confused and then continued to walk towards the wall. There was another flash of light and all at once they were gone. The room was dark, except for the faint blue pulsing in the eyes of the idol. They all stood in silence for a few minutes.

"Are you alright?" Jared nudged Alex on his shoulder. Alex was in a daze. He'd seen Daniel and got the closure he'd wished for. But the emptiness was still there. It would always be there.

"Yeah. I think I am." Alicia walked over and hugged Alex.

"I have an idea." She looked up at Alex.

"Timo, can you turn on your flashlight?"

"Sure." Timo lit up the room with his flashlight.

"I remember this room. We need to go higher up." Alicia pointed to the ceiling.

"The steps are gone," Ron pointed out. Jared produced floating blocks for them to walk on.

"I'll never get used to this!" Timo said excitedly. Alicia picked up the idol. She led the way up the floating stairs.

"Wow!" Alex walked into a large room full of gold artifacts. They were placed throughout the room. The center of the room was barren. The room had a large window facing outside.

"Are we facing the sea?" Jared asked, walking up to the window. The view of the sea below captivated him.

"Jared, can you create a box around us?" He thought about it for a second then nodded yes. He started to fade in a floor. Ron and Timo stepped back, leaving Alex, Jared, and Alicia in the middle of the room. Alicia grabbed both Alex's and Jared's hands, bringing them close. She shifted and held the idol out so that it was directly in the center of the three of them. Alex still wasn't used to seeing her in her all black shifted form. Suddenly, images started to appear on the walls, ceiling, and floor of the box they were in.

"Wow. It's like we're standing in a hologram. Alicia how are you doing this?" Jared asked as they watched the floor become grass and the ceiling become the sky.

171

"I can see things the idol has seen. I can also see what Itzel and Acan have seen." It was the most beautiful place Alex had ever seen. The three of them held hands and watched Acan and Itzel getting married on their home world. They witnessed Itzel crying in her bedroom at the discovery of her fading powers. They saw Isic plotting to overthrow Acan and his leadership. They got to see the council give Acan and Itzel an ultimatum to leave. The people of their world were all gathered together in a great hall. Women and men were crying because their leader Acan and his wife were being forced to leave a planet that they loved. They watched as Acan and Itzel were brought by spaceship to earth. That same spaceship dropped Isic off on a different section of the world. He was pushed out of the ship in disgrace. The soldiers pushed him out of the ship as if he were trash. They watched as that spaceship took off, then blew up shortly after. Isic had watched in satisfaction as the explosive he'd placed on the ship went off, killing every soldier inside. They watched as Acan and Itzel assimilated to their new life in Mexico, while Isic plotted. He used the Awari to create a temple inside of an abandoned cave, and created creatures in secret. His creatures kidnapped innocent people and stole souls to feed the Awari. Once Isic felt strong enough, he had his creatures take Itzel and the townspeople from the village her and Acan had migrated to. Acan came back from hunting to find them missing. He searched the whole village for Itzel, and finally came upon Isic's cave. There he discovered the bloody ceremony Isic had started.

"That was mesmerizing. I felt like I was actually there," Alicia said in wonder. The walls faded away and they were back standing in the center of the room facing the window.

"Thanks for inviting us guys. I can't believe we got to experience this! I don't want to leave this temple," Ron said while Timo stood by the window and took more pictures.

"I have a feeling we'll be seeing more of this temple in the future," Alex walked to the window.

"How do you know that?" Ron asked curiously.

"I can feel it." Alicia and Jared shared a look, and joined Alex at the window. They all stared at the sea below, eyes glowing.

Acknowledgments

I would like to thank Matt, for his support and love; John, for being an amazing, supportive friend of this book; Domonique and Karen for sharing their skills and talent;

Julio and Bob for being my test readers; Felecia and Donna for being inspirations; and those hard times, for making me stronger.

I would also like to thank the readers for reading this story...I hope you like it.

Made in the USA
Middletown, DE
24 December 2021

56953975R00099